A Candlelight Ecstasy Romance™

For the first time Heather felt the searing heat of sheer physical desire. . . .

The kiss went on and on, growing ever more fiery and passionate. Heather felt a totally unfamiliar tide of emotion sweep over her. Her mouth came alive beneath the pressure of his, returning the kiss with hungry urgency. Her rational mind retreated as if he had somehow cast a spell over her. There was pulsating excitement in her veins. Her nerves ran with fire. . . .

D0802838

BREATHLESS SURRENDER

Kay Hooper

A CANDLELIGHT ECSTASY ROMANCE™

Published by
Dell Publishing Co., Inc.
1 Dag Hammarskjold Plaza
New York, New York 10017

ISBN: 0–440–10574–9

Printed in the United States of America
First printing—November 1982

To Our Readers:

We have been delighted with your enthusiastic response to Candlelight Ecstasy Romances™, and we thank you for the interest you have shown in this exciting series.

In the upcoming months we will continue to present the distinctive, sensuous love stories you have come to expect only from Ecstasy. We look forward to bringing you many more books from your favorite authors and also the very finest work from new authors of contemporary romantic fiction.

As always, we are striving to present the unique, absorbing love stories that you enjoy most—books that are more than ordinary romance.

Your suggestions and comments are always welcome. Please write to us at the address below.

Sincerely,

The Editors
Candlelight Romances
1 Dag Hammarskjold Plaza
New York, New York 10017

For A.W. and Dee Robbins,
to keep a promise.
And Clint,
the next generation.

CHAPTER ONE

Chris drew back slowly and stared down at the face of the lovely girl in his arms. The moonlight shining through the car window was bright enough for him to read her expression, and he immediately pulled back from their embrace with a smothered, bitter curse. "That didn't move you at all, did it?" he demanded harshly. "What are you made of, Heather, ice?"

Heather sighed softly. "I'm sorry, Chris, but I can't pretend to feel something that just isn't there."

"Thanks!"

She made a helpless little gesture and then picked up her purse and reached for the door handle. "I'm sorry," she repeated. "I told you from the beginning that we could only be friends."

As she opened the car door Chris said angrily, "I didn't believe the guys at the office when they told me you were a hopeless case, but I sure as hell believe them now! Your nickname suits you perfectly—Ice Princess."

Heather looked at the handsome, boyishly sullen face, and her lips twisted in a faintly wry smile. His anger was the result of wounded pride rather than any deeper emo-

9

tion, and she knew it. Chris Thompson had been bowling women over for the better part of his thirty-five years, and it cut him to the quick to discover a woman who was impervious to his blond good looks and charming smile.

Even though she had warned him a month ago that she wanted no emotional involvement, he had been very determined in his pursuit of her, and she had not been able to discourage him as she had so many others. He had spared no effort to awaken in her a passion as great as his own, but not one of his urgent caresses had struck a responding spark in her veins.

In a detached manner she had felt his sensual expertise to be pleasant, but no more. His caresses had not evoked within her any desire to hop into bed with him—which had been his undisguised intention from the first.

Staring across at him now, Heather wondered rather tiredly if perhaps he wasn't right about her. He was certainly the most gorgeous specimen of American manhood she had encountered during the past year, and God knew most women would have surrendered immediately after a single glimpse of that charming smile. So why hadn't she? Was she frigid?

His voice jerked her from the troubled thoughts. "I mean it, Heather! That beautiful face and sexy body— they're carved out of ice. It would take a blowtorch to get to you," he went on acidly, "and I'm not sure that even that would do the trick!"

She gazed at him for a moment, then said quietly, "Good-bye, Chris." She slid out of the car and shut the door firmly, knowing that he wouldn't be calling her again. The powerful sportscar started with a roar, pulling away from the curb with the tires screaming like an animal in torment. Heather watched the taillights disappear into the darkness and then turned toward her apartment building with a faint sigh.

She let herself in the front door and climbed the stairs

to the second floor. The short, carpeted hallway was lined with half a dozen doors, and muted sounds of music or television programs reached Heather's ears as she made her way to the last door on the right. Hearing the stereo blaring from within, she grimaced slightly and tried the doorknob. It was, as she had expected, unlocked. Pushing the door open, she stepped into the apartment and said immediately, "Lisa, how many times have I warned you to keep this door locked?"

"Damn! Look what you made me do!" The blonde sitting cross-legged on the brown suede couch held up a finger smeared with bright red nail polish. "Honestly, Heather, you're worse than Daddy!" she went on in a voice that was half scornful and half amused. "This building has excellent security, and you know it. There hasn't been a break-in here in years!"

"There's always a first time," Heather retorted, locking the door behind her and coming into the living room. She dropped her purse on the coffee table, then sank down on one of the matching chairs that flanked the couch. "And your father would have a fit if he knew you were parading around the apartment in babydoll pajamas with the drapes open and the door unlocked!"

"I was not parading, I was sitting!" Lisa told her indignantly, busily using a cotton ball soaked in remover to repair the damage to her nail polish. "Oh, blast, I've ruined the other hand. Now I'll have to start all over again."

Heather smiled faintly at the irritated expression of her roommate. "Don't you have anything better to do? I thought you'd still be out. How was the party?"

Lisa rolled her eyes toward heaven expressively. "Lousy. I developed a crashing headache and asked Mike to bring me home. He was very annoyed and pouted the whole way back. I left him at the door without bothering to ask him in for coffee or anything."

The careless tone deepened Heather's smile, and her violet eyes were warm with affection as she gazed at her friend. Lisa had been the object of male attention since her teens, but it had not made her the slightest bit vain. She treated all her admirers in an offhand manner, flirting lightly and never getting serious about any of them. At twenty-four, she was strikingly lovely, tall, and slender, with the perfectly formed features of a high-fashion model.

The two girls were perfect foils for each other, causing heads to turn wherever they went. Heather was petite and raven-haired, her large, black-fringed violet eyes dominating her delicate face. Her tiny waist could easily be spanned by a man's hands, and the remainder of her figure was surprisingly—and eye-catchingly—voluptuous. Needless to say neither young woman lacked admirers, in spite of Lisa's careless manner and Heather's remote one. And they were the best of friends.

Lisa removed the last of the polish and then tossed the used cotton ball onto the glass-topped coffee table. "How was your date?" she asked casually, picking up a bottle of nail polish.

"Fine," Heather replied ruefully, "until we said goodbye."

"Ah!" Lisa immediately looked up, her brown eyes glittering with amusement. "From your expression, I'd hazard a guess that tonight saw another disgruntled suitor bite the dust!"

"Very funny." Heather grimaced slightly.

Lisa burst into a fit of triumphant laughter. "I knew it! I made a bet with Daddy that poor old Chris wouldn't last more than a month."

Heather leaned over to remove her high-heeled shoes. "Your father doesn't gamble," she said absently.

"He'd gamble on you in a heartbeat," Lisa responded flatly. "Just say the word, and I'll be your maid of honor."

In a voice filled with mock horror, Heather said, "And have you as a stepdaughter? Perish the thought!" Hastily she dodged the pillow Lisa threw at her, and then grinned slightly when it struck the stereo and abruptly brought silence to the room. Sitting back in her chair, she said, "Thank God! I was beginning to go deaf!"

There was an unaccustomed frown on Lisa's face. "Seriously, Heather, you know that Daddy adores you. He'd marry you tomorrow if you'd just say the word. Why don't you put him out of his misery? Is it because he's nearly twice your age and has a daughter who *is* your age?"

Heather absently twisted a silver identification bracelet on her wrist. "No. His age doesn't bother me—or your age for that matter," she said quietly. "I'm very fond of Leon, but I'm not in love with him, and it wouldn't be fair to him."

"Daddy doesn't think so," Lisa said softly.

"Well, I do." Heather stared down at the bracelet, still fingering it unconsciously. "Leon's too fine a man to ever have to settle for second best. I couldn't repay him for everything he's done for me by saddling him with a wife who couldn't love him with all her heart."

"You always do that," Lisa said suddenly.

Heather looked up blankly. "Do what?"

"Toy with that bracelet. Whenever something troubles you, you twist it and play with it. Like worry beads or something."

With a slight smile, Heather said lightly, "Some people twirl their hair, some bite their nails; I play with a bracelet."

"You still can't remember who gave it to you?"

"What makes you so sure someone gave it to me?" Heather countered wryly.

"The inscription," Lisa answered with a grin. "You'd

13

hardly buy a bracelet for yourself with an inscription that reads My bright, particular star!"

Heather laughed. "It would be a bit much," she agreed.

"The words sound familiar." Lisa tilted her head to one side thoughtfully. "Is it a quote or something?"

Turning the bracelet so that she could read the back, Heather nodded slowly. "A paraphrase. It's from Shakespeare. 'That I should love a bright, particular star and think to wed it,'" she quoted.

Lisa lifted an eyebrow in surprise. "That sounds serious. Whoever he was, he must have been pretty important to you."

Heather shook her head quickly. "Obviously not—otherwise I'd remember him."

"You probably met him before the accident," Lisa said dryly.

"Yes, before the accident," Heather quietly repeated. And how many times had she heard that phrase, or said it herself, in the past three years? She had almost totally regained her memory, except for that elusive period of about six months. Maybe she would never know what her life had been like during those months, before the accident had nearly ended her life altogether.

Heather shrugged. "Well, after three years, I doubt that I'll ever remember. The psychologist told me that the trauma of the accident caused the memory loss."

Lisa turned the bottle of fingernail polish in her hands, a frown of preoccupation on her face. "Daddy doesn't agree with him though," she murmured. "He thinks that you were running from something—or someone—that night, that something happened to you that you can't bear to remember. It makes sense when you stop to think about it. The police said that your car must have been going like a bat out of hell. There was no luggage in the car, and God only knows what you were doing in Indiana of all places."

Heather shrugged again, frowning herself. "I know. I've

thought about it a lot, but I can't come up with any answers. The only thing that detective could find out was that I quit my job in Los Angeles suddenly, moved out of my apartment without a word to anyone, and vanished. Six months later they found me wrapped around a tree on an Indiana highway."

Three years had dimmed the agony of the accident, so that Heather had no trouble in talking about it. But she could not actually remember the first few weeks after the accident any more than she could remember the six months that had preceded it.

She knew that she had been taken to a hospital where a broken arm and leg had been set; she knew that she had suffered a severe blow to the head that had kept her unconscious for days. She could vaguely remember questions from doctors and police after she had regained consciousness. But she had neither answered them nor completely comprehended what they were asking her. She had been in a strange, apathetic state, obeying orders without comment or question.

She had not spoken to anyone or taken any interest in anything going on around her. After the first few weeks, her memory of the passing days was dreamlike, and it was months before she began to take an interest in living again.

It was not until then, until the mists shrouding her mind had dispersed, that she was able to understand the almost miraculous luck that had befallen her. It was then that she had learned of Dr. Leon Masters's providential visit with a friend and colleague at the Indiana hospital where she had been taken after the accident.

Leon Masters, world-famous for his unequaled skill as a plastic surgeon, had taken one look at the fragile, delicate face, the blank violet eyes, and immediately assumed responsibility for her. The police had been unable to discover her identity. The twisted wreck of the car she had been in had supplied no clue—not even the license plate could be found. Only a silver identification bracelet on one delicate wrist had announced in flowing script that her name was Heather.

Leon had carried her away with him to his private hospital in the mountains of Colorado and, over a period of several months, her mind healed along with her body. And during that time, Leon had fallen in love with her. He had never told her so, but he had not made any attempt to hide his feelings.

Making no demands, he had helped her to piece together the facts of her life, until everything but the six months preceding the accident was clear. Her name was Heather Richards; she was, at that time, twenty-two years old and single. An only child, her parents had died within a few months of each other when she was barely eighteen, and she had been employed as a commercial artist at an advertising agency in Los Angeles six months before the accident.

Still absently fingering the bracelet on her wrist, Heather frowned as she considered the past two years. She had been reluctant to return to Los Angeles and pick up the threads of her former life, and when Leon had suggested that she move in with his daughter in San Francisco instead, she had agreed immediately. She had met Lisa when the lively blonde had visited her father at the hospital, and the two had become fast friends. Heather had been disturbed by Leon's feelings for her, and it was that circumstance more than any other that had caused her to leave the hospital.

She knew that his suggestion that she become his daughter's roommate had its roots in a desire to be able to see her fairly often. Judging by Lisa's wry comments on the subject, he certainly visited his daughter more often than he had in the past, but his behavior toward Heather had been casual and friendly, and she had gradually relaxed. More than once she had been conscious of a wistful

16

desire to be able to return Leon's feelings, but she found it impossible. She was fond of him and certainly grateful for everything he had done for her, but she simply could not love him.

Heather agreed with the psychologist who had visited her often at Leon's hospital: the accident had caused her memory loss. But more than that, it had changed her. She was not the same girl who had mysteriously vanished from L.A. three and a half years before. She was . . . cold. As if the girl she had been was someone else, Heather could remember a fiery temper and ready laughter, a romantic idealism untouched by the cynical realities of the world, a heart which had been, perhaps, too easily touched.

She had been innocent, naive. She had felt very deeply about everything. Untouched by love, she had been eager for it, and at the same time, uncertain, frightened.

And now—to use Chris's description—she seemed carved out of ice. All her emotions were surface ones, and knowing that did nothing to alter it. She could look at Leon with gratitude and affection, but she could not love him. She could date a man she sincerely liked and respected—Chris, for instance—and accept his kisses with a passivity that she could neither fight nor disguise. Her heart beat steadily, pumping life-giving blood through her veins, but it did not ache with sadness or lift in joy. It was as if something within her had died in the accident.

"Hey, snap out of it!" It was Lisa, her voice light. "I didn't mean to bring up bad memories, Heather. Sorry."

Heather smiled faintly, the shadows leaving her violet eyes. "You didn't," she assured her friend. "I went over everything with Dr. Conners so many times that it doesn't bother me anymore. It's just that one thought leads to another—and I end up wondering about those six months."

Lisa sat back on the couch and stretched out her long golden legs, propping her feet upon the coffee table. "It must feel terrible," she said sympathetically, "losing half a year. It would drive me up a wall!"

"No, it wouldn't," Heather responded, her smile widening. "You'd just shrug and tell everyone that you'd managed to misplace six months of your life—and no one would be surprised!"

"Thanks a lot!" The blonde's sober expression melted into laughter. "Anyway, forget about it, Heather, no pun intended. As you said yourself, you're hardly likely to remember now. Unless, of course, someone pops up out of your murky past!"

"Extremely unlikely, I should think," Heather retorted carelessly as she got to her feet. "And now, though you may well be part owl, I am not. I'm going to bed. See you tomorrow."

"Sure. Oh, by the way, Daddy's coming over in the morning. There's some kind of medical conference, and he'll be here all next week. He called from his hotel a couple of hours ago. He said he hoped you hadn't made any plans for tomorrow, because there's something he wants you to see."

"Did he say what it was?" Heather stopped in the doorway leading to her bedroom and frowned slightly, puzzled.

"Nope. He was very mysterious about it, and when I tried to worm the whole thing out of him, he changed the subject and asked if you were seeing Chris tonight. He was very upset when I told him you were."

Dryly, Heather said, "Stop the matchmaking, Lisa. Your father never gets upset over anything. It's one of the nice things about him."

"I don't know," Lisa murmured doubtfully. "Before he met you, I would have agreed with that. I have a feeling, though, that Daddy could get pretty primitive where you're concerned. And he did sound a little—perturbed."

"You're imagining things," Heather scoffed lightly.

18

"I am not. When I told Daddy you were with Chris, there was a full ten seconds of silence, and then he said 'Oh' in the flattest voice imaginable. Then he said he'd be over in the morning, and hung up—abruptly." She nodded wisely. "Perturbed."

Heather sighed. "Lisa—"

"You've broken his spirit," Lisa interrupted in a voice of profound doom. "If you weren't my best friend, I'd make a wax doll in your image and stick pins in it. He's such a nice man. Such a kind man. Fatally obsessed with your unearthly beauty—" She broke off abruptly as Heather's look of weary amusement altered to one of shock. "Hey, I'm just teasing!"

"I know." Heather rubbed the fingers of one hand against her forehead fretfully. "It's just that when you said 'unearthly beauty,' a bell went off. I must have heard it somewhere."

Lisa looked thoughtful. "Your murky past. The guy that gave you that bracelet, probably. After all, he called you his 'bright, particular star'—and stars are certainly unearthly."

Heather laughed suddenly. "Lisa, there is no man in my past! I probably saw the bracelet in a pawnshop somewhere and bought it because it had my name on it."

Lisa shook her head in dissatisfaction. "No way. I just know that bracelet's a key to your past. If we could find out who gave it to you, I'd bet next year's subscription to *Playgirl* that we'd know where you were during that six months."

"You don't even subscribe to *Playgirl*," Heather retorted with another laugh.

"Hush!" Lisa cast a look of mock fear around the apartment. "It's a secret; don't tell Daddy! What would he think of his little girl if he knew?!"

"Good *night*," Heather said firmly.

As her friend started to turn away from her, Lisa abandoned the histrionics abruptly. "Hold it a second! I just remembered something else."

"Am I never to get to bed?" Heather demanded in despair and then went on quickly, "never mind! Whatever it is, it'll keep until tomorrow." She disappeared into her bedroom.

"Don't you want to hear about your new boss?" Lisa sang out sweetly.

Heather came out of her bedroom somewhat faster than she'd gone in, only the top button of her blouse unfastened. "New boss? What new boss?" she asked blankly.

"I thought that would get your attention."

Coming farther into the room, Heather stared at her roommate in bewilderment. "I know I've been on vacation the past week, but don't try to tell me the whole office fell apart without me! What's happened, for heaven's sake?"

Lisa laughed. "Not quite that, but there have been some drastic changes. I didn't hear about it until today, because I've been in and out all week shooting that layout for the new cosmetics account."

Heather frowned slightly and waited for her to go on, wondering why her boss had not mentioned the matter to her. She was, after all, the secretary and assistant to James Norden. Norden Advertising was his baby, his whole life, and she couldn't see him calmly handing over the reins to someone else.

She and Lisa both worked for the company. Lisa was not—as her looks seemed to indicate—a model, but a talented photographer. She had been there for two years when Heather moved in with her, and it had seemed natural for Heather to apply for a job with Norden. He had wanted to hire her as a commercial artist, but she had told him calmly that she wanted to be a secretary, and since his own secretary was leaving to marry, he had hired her.

Lisa grimaced faintly. "From what I could gather, Norden's doctor warned him that he was heading for a heart attack if he didn't slow down immediately. Well, you know Norden—nothing by half measures. He knew darn well it wouldn't be possible for him to slow down, so he got out entirely. He sold the company."

Heather's violet eyes widened in astonishment. "Sold the company? Outright?"

With a nod, Lisa went on. "Scuttlebutt has it that he passed the word around last weekend, and a buyer turned up on the doorstep Monday morning. Oh, not literally," she added as Heather's eyes widened even more. "Lawyers and things," she murmured cryptically. "Anyway, the deal was apparently settled today."

"Fast work," Heather commented slowly. "But what about the staff, the employees?"

Lisa shrugged. "We're part of the deal apparently. According to what I heard, Norden was very firm on that. So unless someone makes a horrendous boo-boo or forgets to bow and scrape, we stay."

Heather came forward to lean against the back of a chair, her ears immediately picking up the faintly derisively note in Lisa's voice. "Bow and scrape? Is the new boss a tyrant, or what?"

"God knows." Lisa frowned and stared into space. "Bear in mind that my sources couldn't exactly be considered one hundred percent accurate—gossip never is. And the moment the buyer's name filtered through the ranks, gossip ran riot."

Impatiently Heather said, "Well, tell me what you've heard."

"Okay. Enter Adam Blake. His family have been in advertising for years in New York, but for some reason— undiscovered as yet—he was never crazy about the business. Rumor has it that he quarreled violently with his father when the old man wanted him to step into his shoes, but that could well be pure fabrication. Anyway, the fact is that he did take over the company when his father had a bad accident and wound up in a wheelchair. That was about twelve years ago, after Adam graduated from college."

"And since then?" Heather asked curiously.

Lisa grinned. "He's been making a name for himself—and I don't just mean businesswise! You know the type. He jets around the world, has a woman in every port—or at least he did."

Heather lifted a quizzical brow. "Did?"

"Mmmm." Lisa nodded. "One of the girls in the typing pool—Sharon, I think—went to the library and dug up some old newspaper clippings about him. According to her, he shocked the business community of New York by dropping out of sight suddenly a few years ago. The press was wildly curious about the whole thing, but the old buzzard—I mean Daniel Blake"—she corrected herself hurriedly—"didn't explain. He just took over the company again and acted as though his son didn't exist."

Heather perched on the arm of the chair she had been leaning against and frowned slightly. "That doesn't make sense."

"It's weird, isn't it?" Lisa shrugged. "The scandal sheets made a lot of noise about a family feud over some woman, but no one could find out anything for certain. Adam Blake returned to New York—if he'd ever left!—more than a year later, and picked up the reins of the company again. Daniel Blake went back into retirement, and neither of them explained a thing."

Lisa leaned forward suddenly, her brown eyes intent. "There's one thing I know for certain though. *Something* happened during that year, something so awful that it caused an irreparable breach between Daniel and Adam Blake."

Heather's eyes widened at this dramatic pronouncement. "How do you know that, Lisa?"

"That rotten party tonight, remember?" She waited for

her friend's nod before going on. "Well, I met this guy. He's a free-lance artist, and he worked for Blake's company a few years ago. He wasn't there when Adam vanished, but he was there when he returned. Skip—that's his name; perfect for an artist, don't you think?—says that there was a terrible fight between Blake and his son. It was heard practically all over the building. Daniel was roaring something about Adam ruining his life over some scheming little slut, and Adam was yelling right back that he was taking the business over again only because he didn't want his father's death on his conscience."

"That sounds awfully bitter," Heather remarked slowly, then shook her head. "I don't think I should be hearing this, Lisa. His private life's no concern of mine, after all."

"It is too," Lisa said stoutly. "You'll be working very closely with Adam Blake; you should know everything you can about him. Besides," she went on, "you haven't heard the rest."

Involuntarily Heather asked, "There's more?"

With a nod, Lisa said, "According to Skip, that was the last time that Adam and his father saw each other. Ever since that day, they've only communicated through business associates and lawyers. Skip didn't stay with the company very long after that, but he says that the employees there couldn't get over how much Adam Blake had changed since he'd come back. Before he disappeared, he was always getting in the papers with some model or actress, but after he came back, there weren't any women."

Heather looked startled. "None at all?"

"Unless he was very, very discreet, none at all," Lisa affirmed. "And what Sharon said bears that out, Heather. After he took over the company for the second time, he seemed to bury himself in his work. No more jet-setting, no more all-night parties. Nothing. Sharon checked the clippings very carefully, but there wasn't a single mention of a woman in connection with Adam Blake after that year."

With a slight smile, Heather murmured, "Maybe he was crossed in love."

"In my experience," Lisa responded with a faint grimace, "men who have been crossed in love don't wrap themselves in their work because of it. They're far more likely to go on a binge!"

"Such *vast* experience," Heather mocked softly.

"Well, they do! I've seen it happen too. A man gets disillusioned over a woman, and the next thing you know, he's hopping from bed to bed all over town, trying to forget her."

The bitter note in her friend's voice caused Heather to look at her closely. "Lisa?" she probed gently.

Lisa avoided the searching gaze. "Anyway, Adam has a younger brother who's old enough to take over the New York company now, so he's apparently decided to expand to the West Coast, probably to get away from his father."

"Never mind Adam Blake," Heather dismissed impatiently. "Tell me what's bothering you."

Lisa was silent for a long moment, then burst out suddenly, "Unrequited love is so boring!" She shook her head. "You don't want to hear about it."

"Yes, I do," Heather insisted quietly. "Tell me."

Continuing to stare straight in front of her, Lisa said dully, "Alexander Sinclair. Remember him?"

"I remember," Heather responded, trying to conceal her shock. Both she and Leon had been relieved, weeks before, when Lisa had stopped seeing Sinclair, who was the closest thing to an eighteenth-century English rake San Francisco could boast of, and fifteen years Lisa's senior into the bargain.

Lisa shrugged wearily. "I didn't take him seriously. I

24

mean, who would? He's the playboy of the West Coast, for God's sake! I told him at the start that I had no intention of becoming one of his little playmates, and he knew I meant it." With a ragged sigh, she went on slowly. "He was different from any of the other men I've dated. It wasn't because he was so much older, experienced, and wealthy. That wasn't it at all. He . . . he treated me like a *queen*!" She grimaced suddenly. "That sounds utterly fatuous, I know, but it's the truth."

"When did you realize you loved him?"

"I didn't. I mean, oh, hell!" she muttered. "It's hard to explain. I thought he was just amusing himself with me, that he'd get bored pretty soon, so I treated the whole thing very casually. It didn't occur to me that he was serious. But then he proposed, Heather."

"Marriage?"

Lisa gave a choked little laugh. "It surprised me too. I—I didn't believe him. Until that moment, I hadn't let myself think about how I felt toward him, but when he asked me to marry him . . ." Her voice trailed off.

"You wanted to say yes?"

Lisa nodded unhappily. "More than anything in the world. But I was afraid to. It just didn't seem possible that he could love me. I convinced myself that he was playing some sort of cruel trick on me, and I . . . Oh, God, Heather, I was such a bitch! I said awful things, like never having any peace because I wouldn't know whose bed he was in, and then I told him to get lost. And he did. He did, damn him!"

After a moment, Heather said very quietly, "Have I been so blind, Lisa? You've been hurting all these weeks, and I never noticed."

Her friend managed a shaky, though reassuring smile. "It wasn't so bad at first. I kept telling myself that he'd call, or I'd see him somewhere. But tonight I saw him,

Heather. He was with Teri Evans. Remember her?"
Heather nodded silently, and Lisa went on miserably.
"She's perfect for him. Beautiful, intelligent, cultured, and
nearer to his own age. I can't even hate her, Heather. It's
been common knowledge for years that she's in love with
him. Whenever he breaks up with a woman, he starts
dating Teri—until the next woman comes along."

There was a long silence, and then Heather said slowly,
"You said something about hopping from bed to bed. Did
you mean that literally?"

Lisa nodded. Rather bitterly she said, "You know how
people are always eager to tell you about your ex-lover. He
was never my lover—not literally anyway—but no one
would ever believe that. With his reputation it's under-
standable."

"You mean that people have been cruel enough to tell
you things about Alex's women?"

The faint note of shock in Heather's voice brought a
genuine smile to her friend's face. "In some ways, Heather, you're as innocent as a babe," she murmured fondly.
"You can never understand cruelty in people." With a soft
sigh, she went on wryly. "Of course they told me. No one
from the office, thank God. I made sure Alex never picked
me up there. But others, people we both know socially.
Oh, it was all done very casually, very sweetly. Usually the
remarks weren't even addressed to me. But they were
meant for me."

"What kind of remarks?"

Lisa drew her knees up and propped her chin on them.
"Oh, that Alex Sinclair had been seen dining with a different woman every night, that he had a weekend guest who
wore diamonds, that he bought a bright red sportscar for
some unnamed redhead and a sapphire necklace for a
blue-eyed blonde. That sort of thing."

"Sportscar? Sapphire necklace?" Heather shook her

head dazedly. "Lisa, did he . . . did he ever buy you anything like that?"

She shook her head. "No." Bitterly she went on. "I'm sure he didn't get rich by paying for services *not* rendered."

"Lisa!"

"Well!" Lisa shook her head impatiently. "Look, I don't want to believe all the gossip I've heard, but I can't ignore it. And I can't go crawling to Alex and tell him that I've made a mistake. He could very well laugh in my face, and that would kill me. Obviously he isn't eating his heart out for me."

Very quietly Heather asked, "And what if all the gossip is false?"

Lisa lifted bleak eyes to her friend. "I can't take the chance. I'm too afraid of being hurt."

Heather sighed softly. "You're hurting now, Lisa. Would it be any worse to know for sure?"

Lisa sat in silence for a long time and then shook her head as if throwing off a disturbing thought. She got to her feet. "Maybe not," she conceded quietly, "but I don't want to know for sure. Not right now. Later, when I think I can take it." She grinned faintly. "Thanks for letting me bend your ear anyway."

"I wish I could do more," Heather murmured.

With a rueful gesture, Lisa said, "We all have to do our own hurting, you know. No one can hurt for us. See you in the morning, Heather."

"Good night." Heather watched her friend go into her bedroom and then turned off the lamp and went into her own room. As she got undressed, she thought about Lisa and Alex and wondered if perhaps she and Leon hadn't been a little too quick to condemn. If Alex had proposed, then he obviously cared a great deal for Lisa. There had never been even the faintest hint of a rumor that Alex

Sinclair had ever considered marriage before.

Perhaps there was something more she could do after all. . . .

Her last thought before dropping off to sleep was to wonder what Leon's surprise was.

CHAPTER TWO

Heather sat silently on the passenger side of the small rented car, her eyes on the hawklike profile of the man at her side. He was a distinguished-looking man, Leon Masters, with his daughter's intelligent brown eyes and warm smile. At forty-eight his hair was more silver than blond, and the passage of time had etched deep lines around his eyes and alongside his nose and mouth. He carried his six-foot height with ease, his lean body fit and hard, without an ounce of surplus fat.

He was a complicated man, Heather thought as she studied the deceptively arrogant profile, a man whose most important goal in life was to restore beauty to faces ravaged by illness and accident. He looked like a hard, uncaring man, the brown eyes capable of assuming a certain frosty disdain on those rare occasions when he was roused to anger. He never shouted; in fact, his normal speaking voice was quiet and gentle and inexpressibly soothing.

He was, quite simply, the kindest man Heather had ever known in her life.

Wrapped in thought, Heather blinked suddenly as she

realized that they had apparently reached their destination. Leon was parking the car on the side of the road, expertly cramping the wheels against the curb of the steep hill. She glanced around, amused to note an impromptu guitar concert going on across the street. Then Leon had come around to her side of the car and opened the door, and she hurriedly got out.

She waited until they were on the sidewalk and moving among the thick stream of weekend shoppers before asking the question that she had asked several times already. "Leon, where are we going?"

"You'll see."

Heather resisted an impulse to sigh with faint irritation. It was the same answer. Leon seemed determined not to satisfy her curiosity until they reached wherever it was they were going. She looked at her escort, a faint frown appearing between her brows. For the most part, they walked without touching, but occasionally Leon would catch her elbow to steer her around some pedestrian who would not move. It was during those brief moments of physical contact that Heather sensed an unusual tension in Leon, a strange anxiety which was as unfathomable as it was out of character.

"Leon?" She slipped a hand inside the crook of his arm. "Is something wrong?"

He looked down at her quickly, the lines of strain on his face immediately smoothing out. Smiling easily, he replied, "Wrong? No, of course not."

He was lying, Heather knew. Leon had never been able to lie very well. The evidence was there in his eyes. They were guarded, secretive, and wary. Heather felt a strange little chill of fear as she stared at him, and Leon seemed to sense it. He patted the hand resting on his arm comfortingly.

"There's nothing, really. I just have a little surprise for you, that's all."

She forgot the instant of fear. Like a child, she was eager for an unexpected surprise. "Lisa said you were being mysterious!" she exclaimed. "What is it, Leon?"

"Something I want you to see."

"What?" She tugged at his arm playfully. "Come on, Leon, tell me."

"I'd rather show you. Here we are." With his free hand he gestured slightly to indicate a doorway they were approaching.

Heather looked quickly and then stopped dead in her tracks, violet eyes widening as she read the flowing letters above the door.

"We're blocking traffic." Leon's gentle voice seem to come from a very great distance.

Heather blinked and became aware of the people passing on either side of them on the busy sidewalk. In a brittle voice she said, "Leon, you know I can't go in there. That's an art gallery."

"I know, Heather. Trust me." He gently squeezed the trembling hand resting on his arm.

She stared at him almost blindly. Since the accident she had made no attempt to use her God-given artistic talent. When Leon's detective had discovered Heather's former career, both the psychologist and Leon had suggested that sketching would be therapeutic for her. But she had become unusually agitated by the suggestion, refusing to even touch a sketch pad. Heather was completely at a loss to explain her agitation, just as she could not understand her curious aversion to make use of a talent she had once gloried in.

But so it was. And her aversion included a marked antipathy for anyplace likely to contain art or artists. She avoided galleries like the plague, and could not be induced to even enter the art department at work. The girls in the office called it a phobia; Heather was inclined to agree.

"Leon, I can't. You know I can't. We tried once before,

remember? In Denver. I—I couldn't breathe. It felt as if the walls were closing in on me." Her voice was thin, frightened.

"It will be different this time, Heather, I promise." His hand tightened on hers. "This is a very large gallery, and the painting I want you to see is just inside the door." Without giving her a chance to respond, he drew her forward.

Heather gritted her teeth and tried to fight off the terrible smothering feeling that closed in on her the moment Leon led her through the doors. Then they were inside, and her eyes automatically followed Leon's pointing finger.

Immediately the suffocating sensation was gone, replaced by sheer shock. She was unconscious of being led forward, unaware of Leon's reassuring grip on her fingers. The only thing that seemed real to her was the painting they were approaching.

Standing before the portrait, she was vaguely aware that it was the focal point of the entire huge room, vaguely aware that people were staring and whispering, but it didn't matter. She released Leon's arm and stepped closer to the painting, her eyes huge.

It was, and yet was not, herself. The raven-haired, violet-eyed girl in the portrait was full of life and laughter and love. Her violet eyes gleamed with a mixture of humor and teasing, almost unconscious seduction. The delicate pink lips were curved in a tiny smile, pouting slightly, clearly inviting the kiss of a lover.

The girl was half-turned to the artist, one small, slender hand holding the lapels of the purple silk robe together over her full breasts, the other hand resting on the lounge just behind her hips. The robe, unfastened and half falling from her shoulders, was clearly her only clothing. It covered enough of her so that by no stretch of the imagination could it be considered indecent, but it left enough bare—

white shoulders, the tops of creamy breasts, one slender leg raised and resting casually on the lounge—to leave a decidedly erotic impression on those viewing it.

For a single brief moment out of time the gallery disappeared and Heather *was* the girl in the portrait. Vague, dreamlike, she felt herself turning on the lounge to scold the man behind the easel for placing her in such a seductive pose. The easel came into her view, and then . . .

The gallery returned. Heather swayed slightly and felt Leon catch her arm to steady her. Like a bubble, the faint surge of memory had vanished.

"Heather?"

She turned automatically to meet his intent, searching eyes, realizing now why he had not warned her. She would not have come. Like a child terrified of some inexplicable something in the dark, she had always been wary of probing the six-month void in her past.

"Heather? Do you remember posing for the portrait?"

She stared at him for a moment. "No." Her eyes swung immediately back to the portrait, her mind jolting at the realization that this was the first time she had ever lied to Leon. She had remembered. For a brief moment she had remembered.

"It *is* you, Heather. You posed for that picture sometime before the accident." He gestured slightly to the painting.

Heather didn't need the gesture to point out something that was obvious. Her hand rose absently to finger the tiny, crescent-shaped scar high on her right cheek, the only physical reminder of her accident.

The girl in the painting had no scar.

Almost feverishly Heather's eyes searched the painting for the signature of the artist. She found it in the lower lefthand corner. A single word, scrawled untidily, slanting backward: Hyde.

33

"Hyde? I—I've never heard of him. Who is he?"

Leon sighed. "That's something I can't find out. I talked to Andrews, the owner of this gallery, when I first saw the portrait yesterday. He told me that he wasn't free to give out any information about the artist; he wouldn't even tell me if the man's here in San Francisco. He just said that this painting wasn't for sale at any price. Period."

"Maybe he'd talk to me. Do you think he would?"

Leon studied her intently. "Are you sure you want to find out anything about this portrait, Heather?"

She avoided his eyes. "That's a ridiculous question, Leon. Of course I want to find out. Why wouldn't I?"

"You've been hiding," he told her flatly. "For three years, you've been hiding. I think you're afraid to remember what happened during those six months."

Heather stared at him in surprise. Leon's voice had been unusually harsh, his expression taut. It was almost as if he were angry with her. But why? "I—I have tried to remember. You know I have. But it's just blank."

His brown eyes bored into hers for a long moment in a hard, searching stare. Then he released a heavy sigh. "Let's go and find Andrews. He must be in his office; I don't see him around."

When he started to take her arm, Heather stepped back and shook her head. "No, you wait here, Leon. He might be more willing to talk to me if I'm alone."

Leon opened his mouth to protest, hesitated, and then nodded. "Maybe you're right. Follow that hall leading off to the right. His office is the last door on the left."

Leaving him standing in front of the painting, Heather made her way through the crowded gallery. She was painfully aware of the stares she was receiving but managed to ignore them until she reached the hall that Leon had indicated. Two men were standing by the hall, and Heather recognized them vaguely as being two artists who were employed by Norden. She gave them a polite nod and then moved on.

She located Andrews's office with no trouble at all. The door was standing ajar. She knocked lightly and, hearing no one, pushed the door open and went in. It was a fairly small office, almost entirely occupied by a large oak desk. The top of the desk was cluttered. Various notices of art shows and exhibits were tacked onto a bulletin board occupying an entire wall. But no Andrews.

Heather sighed, turned to leave, and found her way barred by a very large masculine body. Automatically she looked up, and the breath caught in her throat with an audible gasp.

The stranger didn't look surprised at her reaction, and Heather could easily understand why. He must have heard many women gasp when they looked at him. It wasn't enough that he was well over six feet tall with broad, powerful shoulders tapering to a lean waist and narrow hips, or that thick black hair, lightly silvered at the temples, crowned his arrogant head. That would have been enough for any man. But nature had apparently taken a great deal of pleasure in gilding this particular lily.

The face that Heather stared at with unconscious fascination was the answer to every woman's dream. Deeply tanned, it was lean and strong, with high cheekbones and a determined jaw. Black brows, like definitive strokes of an artist's brush, slanted upward toward his silvered temples in a curiously bold manner. His eyes were an unfathomable black, like polished jet. The nose was perfect, his lips beautifully molded and sensuous.

And those lips were smiling now with amusement as he studied the delicate face turned up to his. The smile jerked Heather back to an awareness of her surroundings, and she hastily lowered her eyes, a sudden flush darkening her cheeks. Instinct told her that he was not the man she had

35

come in search of. "Excuse me," she murmured, and stepped aside to go around him.

He turned slightly, a powerful, long-fingered hand coming out to grasp the doorjamb, blocking her passage. Heather found herself staring fixedly at the silver medallion nestling amid the dark hair on his chest, painfully aware that his cream-colored shirt was unbuttoned almost to the waist. She seemed oddly unable to think properly, nearly hypnotized by the way the medallion shimmered in the light as his muscular chest rose and fell slowly.

"I said excuse me," she said breathlessly.

His only response was to step toward her, and Heather backed away as if he had made a violently threatening gesture. He came far enough into the room to close the door and then leaned back against it, staring at her from beneath sleepy lids. "They call you the Ice Princess," he drawled softly.

She swallowed and then said as coldly as she could manage, "I don't know who you are, but if you don't open that door and let me out, I'll scream the place down!"

"You don't sound very sure," he mocked in a soft, deep voice.

Heather shivered without knowing why, bewildered by the odd effect this stranger was having on her senses. "I—I am sure," she responded, silently cursing the break in her voice. "And I mean it. I'll scream."

"Oh, no, you won't, sweet Heather."

She took another involuntary step backward, coming up against the desk. "How do you know my name?"

He smiled, showing strong, even white teeth. "I overheard a couple of guys talking out there." A slight jerk of his dark head indicated the gallery. "They called you Heather, the Ice Princess, the woman no man can thaw."

She stiffened, realizing that the two men from Norden had been discussing her. Before she could speak, the stranger did.

36

"That's a challenge no redblooded man could ignore. I thought I'd have a shot at it."

Heather felt the first stirrings of panic. "I—I don't know what you're talking about," she managed unsteadily.

He stepped toward her, a strange, feverish glow in the black eyes. "I think you do, Heather," he murmured huskily.

Heather had no opportunity to voice the protest rising in her throat; she was given no chance to move away from him. Within the space of a heartbeat, she was jerked against the solid wall of his chest, her wrists pinned at the small of her back by one of his hands.

A treacherous weakness invaded her lower limbs as she felt the strength of his thighs pressed against her. An odd tremor that was half excitement and half fear spread through her body. She was confused by the unfamiliar sensations rushing along her nerve endings and frightened by the strange glow in his eyes. The fear kept her silent and still in his embrace, and she looked up with wide, blank eyes as his dark head lowered to hers.

His lips moved gently, persuasively over hers, and it took every ounce of control Heather could muster to remain passive beneath his touch. Anger and dismay warred within her as that realization penetrated. She kept her mouth firmly closed against him, aware that something was melting inside her and she was disturbed by the implications of that. This man . . . this *stranger* . . .

He laughed softly against her lips. "Open your mouth, Heather," he whispered. "Let me in."

"You go to—" she began furiously.

It was what he had been waiting for. Immediately the firm lips captured hers again, no longer gentle but hungry and demanding. His tongue intruded with shattering sensuality, exploring the sweetness of her mouth. He released her wrists, his right hand remaining at the small of her back, pressing her closer to his hard length. His left hand moved caressingly against her throat, warm and oddly shaky.

For the first time in her memory, Heather felt the searing heat of sheer physical desire. Her nerves ran with fire, there was a pulsing excitement in her veins. Her rational mind retreated as if he had somehow cast a spell over her. Her mouth came alive beneath the pressure of his, returning the kiss with hungry urgency. Slender arms crept unknowingly around his neck.

The kiss went on and on, growing ever more fiery and passionate. Heather felt a totally unfamiliar tide of emotion sweep over her, finally knowing what it was to want a man, to feel primitive need clawing inside her like a living thing desperate to escape. The ice she had encased herself in fell away from her with a suddenness that was devastating.

When he finally drew away from her, Heather was dizzy and breathless. She hardly noticed when he gently removed her arms from around his neck. Vaguely she was aware that she was leaning heavily against the desk behind her, because her legs were quite literally incapable of supporting her. It didn't matter. The spell remained.

The stranger stared down into her dazed violet eyes, his own a little clouded. He reached out slowly to brush the back of his hand lightly down on her flushed cheek, hesitating almost imperceptibly at the tiny scar, and then traced the tremulous, swollen curve of her lips with a gentle finger. "Sweet Heather," he breathed almost soundlessly. "The name suits you—a tiny, wild flower. Who would suspect that beneath that beautiful, remote exterior lurked so much fire?"

Hardly aware of speaking, Heather whispered, "Who are you?"

Impossibly his eyes seemed to darken even more, and Heather felt vaguely that she could easily lose herself in that seductive, velvety blackness. "Who do you want me to be?" he asked softly, hypnotically.

She stared at him, seeing a lion in summer, black-maned and proud. There was something dangerous about him, in his eyes, in his stance. He was a man to be wary of, and every instinct Heather possessed screamed a warning. But it was too late. Dimly she was somehow aware that it had been too late from the moment she had first set eyes on him. "I—do I know you?"

He laughed under his breath. "You will, sweet Heather." The words were a command, a plea, a promise. "You will."

The quiet click of the door being shut behind him broke the spell that had held Heather immobile. She blinked, her mind suddenly clear. Staring at the closed door, she felt a wave of heat sweeping up her face. "It was just a kiss!" she told the silent room defiantly. *Just a kiss?* her mind objected scornfully. *That's like saying that Vesuvius is just a molehill!*

It was several moments before Heather could trust herself to meet Leon's keen eyes with something approaching her normal calm. She was both bewildered and a little frightened by her response to the stranger, but she pushed that to the back of her mind. She would think about it later, she promised herself. Once she was home, she would lie back on her bed and ask herself why the stranger had awakened this strange restlessness within her. Later.

Approaching Leon, Heather was unaware that her cheeks were softly flushed, her lips tremulous. A glow was in her eyes that he had never seen before. She was unaware that the change within her body had wrought an equal change without.

"Did he tell you who the artist is?" Leon asked.

For a moment Heather didn't know what he was talking about. Her eyes shifted in confusion, settling finally on the portrait. "No," she murmured. "He wasn't in his office."

"You didn't see him at all?" Leon tried and failed to read her expression.

"No." She stared at the painting, her feigned interest in it suddenly becoming real. "Leon, have you noticed the bracelet?"

Leon, frowning, studied her for a moment, then turned his gaze to the painting. "Oh, you mean because it's on the left arm? Yes, I noticed that yesterday."

"I wonder why," Heather mused, fingering the bracelet on her right wrist. "I've worn it on the right arm since the accident, and I don't remember having it before then."

He shrugged slightly. "Probably a simple explanation. The artist may have told you what arm to wear it on."

She started to respond, then hesitated as a peculiar chill ran down her spine. A flickering glance showed her that Leon's attention was focused on the painting, so she felt free to glance guardedly around the room.

He was standing a few short feet away, arms folded across his chest as he leaned against a wall. And he was staring at her. The black eyes were mocking, insolent, moving down her body with cool, deliberate slowness. His gaze had the impact of a physical caress, and Heather gasped in shock when her body responded to his look the way it had responded to his touch.

She tore her eyes away from the handsome, mocking face just in time to meet Leon's concerned gaze, attracted by her soft gasp.

"Heather, are you all right? You're a bit flushed."

She searched feverishly in her mind for an excuse and finally settled on the tried and true. "The—the gallery's beginning to bother me. Could we go home now, Leon?"

"Of course." He put an arm around her shoulders and led her from the gallery, never noticing the man who watched them both with brooding, unreadable eyes.

Later in the apartment Heather faced Leon with a look of faint accusation in her eyes. "Some surprise."

40

Leon sank down on the couch and lit one of his infrequent cigarettes. He stared fixedly at the glowing end of the cigarette for a long moment, then looked up at her with a shrug. "I thought it might jar your memory. And you did remember something, didn't you?"

Heather sat down on the other end of the couch. Disregarding the question, she muttered, "You should have warned me."

"Answer the question, Heather. Did you remember something?"

"Don't push me!" she flared suddenly, her nerves ragged. "Don't you understand? It's like walking into an unfamiliar room in total darkness, not knowing what I'll see when the lights come on!"

His jaw tightened. "You *did* remember then."

She slumped, staring down at her folded hands. "I don't know," she responded dully. "There was something, and then . . . I don't know." Vaguely she wondered if the painting had thrown her off balance. Was that why she had responded to the stranger?

Very quietly Leon said, "Stop fighting it, Heather."

She stared at him in bewilderment. "Fighting it? I'm not fighting anything. What are you talking about, Leon?"

Leon bent forward to crush his cigarette out in an ashtray on the coffee table almost savagely. "You're fighting not to remember," he told her harshly. "But you have to remember, Heather. Sooner or later you have to remember."

"Remember what?" She looked at him with unconsciously pleading eyes. "That I once looked at a man with love in my eyes?"

He avoided her gaze. "I don't know. But the answer is somewhere in your mind."

She lowered her eyes to the bracelet on her wrist, absently noticing that she was fingering it again. "I don't feel

41

as if I've ever been in love," she murmured almost inaudibly.

"But you don't feel free, do you?"

It seemed an odd question, and Heather turned it over in her mind. Was that the reason she had never felt any response to a man since the accident, because she didn't feel herself to be free? Did some deeply buried knowledge constantly warn her that she was not free to love a man?

But what about the stranger? Had she responded to him only because seeing the painting had awakened some cord of memory within her, jarred a door long closed and locked?

Yes, that had to be it. The stranger had simply come along at the right—or wrong—time. And the flicker of memory she had felt, her response to the stranger's touch —were they the first steps to regaining her memory? Would she find it easy to remember now?

She concentrated, trying to break through the barriers her mind had erected after the accident. It was no good. Her attempts to remember bounced off the locked door in her mind until she felt dizzy and sick. Because she was still torn emotionally, she knew, still uncertain. A part of her didn't want to remember, fearing the pain that such knowledge would surely bring. A part of her cried insistently that it was vital, absolutely vital, that she remember.

"Heather?"

She looked up, meeting Leon's worried eyes, and tried to recall his question. "Oh, yes, you're right. I don't feel free."

"Do you want to? Feel free, I mean?"

Another odd question. Heather didn't feel like considering the implications of it. She was too tired. "Leon, if you don't mind, I'd like to be alone for a while."

He stared at her for a moment and then nodded. "If that's what you want. I'll call later to see how you're feeling." He rose and started for the door, then hesitated. "Heather, you won't do anything silly, will you?"

She looked at him with weary, puzzled eyes. "Silly? What do you mean by that, Leon?"

"Never mind," he muttered after a moment. "I'll talk to you later." Silently he left the apartment.

Heather absently kicked her shoes off and curled her legs beneath her on the couch. She brushed Leon's last question from her mind. It didn't seem important, not when there were so many other questions to be answered.

When Lisa returned from photographing a fashion show several hours later, Heather was in the kitchen preparing to put a steak under the broiler. "Have you eaten?" she called out to her roommate. "I didn't know if you were going out tonight, but there's another steak if you want it."

"I want it." Lisa came into the kitchen after dropping her huge tote bag in the living room. "There's some party or other tonight, but I really don't feel much like—" She broke off abruptly as she got a good look at Heather, her eyes widening.

Heather turned to stare at her friend, puzzled by the sudden silence. From the way Lisa was staring at her, anyone would think she'd suddenly sprouted another head. She glanced down at the floral caftan she was wearing, her expression bewildered. "What is it?"

Lisa leaned against the counter, casual in jeans and a western-style shirt. With her eyes fixed on Heather's face, she said dryly, "I don't know what Daddy's surprise was, but it sure must have been something."

"What makes you say that?"

"You look," Lisa murmured thoughtfully, "like a different person. Glowing. Did Daddy pop the question, or what?"

Heather smiled slightly and turned to take another steak from the refrigerator. "No, he didn't pop the question. And stop even thinking things like that. Leon knows I don't feel that way about him. He just wanted to show me something, that's all." Absently she wondered if she really looked so different. Had the painting affected her so much, or was the stranger responsible?

"Well?" Lisa sounded impatient. "Heather, for God's sake, tell me what it was before I die of curiosity!"

Heather put both steaks under the broiler and then turned to face her friend. "It was a painting," she responded in an offhand voice. "A painting in a gallery."

"I think I'd better sit down." Lisa moved to the small dinette table and pulled out a chair. "You mean Daddy actually got you inside a gallery? That must have been some painting!"

With a rueful smile Heather sat down across from her at the table. "It was," she confessed wryly. "It was a portrait, Lisa, a portrait of me."

Without a moment's hesitation Lisa exclaimed, "Your memory loss! The portrait has something to do with your memory loss, doesn't it?"

Heather sighed, irritably pushing the stranger from her mind. "It was painted sometime before the accident, that much I'm sure of. I think your father believes it was painted during that six months."

"What do you think?"

Frowning, Heather replied, "I agree. I don't remember posing for it, but when I first looked at it, I felt something." She shook her head. "A flash of memory, I suppose. For a split second, I was *there*, turning to speak to the artist. And then nothing."

Excitedly Lisa said, "The artist! He could tell you—"

Heather shook her head. "The owner of the gallery said that he wasn't free to give out information about the artist. The only thing we know is that his name is Hyde. Leon called a few minutes ago and said that he couldn't find anyone—*anyone*—in San Francisco who knows anything

44

about him. He checked all the galleries, talked to a few artists. Nothing. I even called the library and had them check *Who's Who.*" She shrugged. "No listing."

Lisa looked astonished. "This is the first time I've ever heard of an artist who didn't want to be known," she muttered. "Usually they're overflowing with ego."

Heather grinned faintly. "Then Hyde's an oddity."

With a curious frown Lisa murmured, "Why do I get the feeling that all the answers are right in front of us if we only had the sense to know what we're looking for?"

Amused, Heather asked, "What do you mean by that?"

"It doesn't strike you as odd?" When her friend continued to look puzzled, Lisa went on slowly. "That painting turning up here in San Francisco of all places. Why? You never lived here before the accident. And an artist who doesn't want recognition? Again, why?" She looked inquisitively at Heather. "Is the painting good? I mean, does Hyde have talent?"

Heather leaned an elbow on the table and frowned reflectively. "Well, it's not easy to be objective when the subject's yourself." She remembered the startlingly lifelike portrait, remembered the emotions that had been portrayed so vividly. Looking up to find Lisa watching her questioningly, she sighed. "America's answer to Michelangelo," she answered simply.

Startled, Lisa exclaimed, "He's that good?"

With no hesitation Heather murmured, "Brilliant. But that's only my opinion, you know."

"Yes, but you've had training in art. You know what's good and what's not." She shook her head slowly. "Good Lord! And the man doesn't want to be known? That's insane!"

Heather made a helpless little gesture. "I can't explain it. I can't even explain why we're all assuming the artist is a man. For all we know, it could be a little old lady from Boston!"

"No way," Lisa said immediately. "Hyde has to be a man; women never paint women."

Heather laughed suddenly. "There's probably something wrong with that statement, but I don't know what it is!"

Lisa smiled in response but appeared to be lost in thought. After a moment she murmured, "It's an interesting little puzzle. I only wish we had all the pieces. I've got a feeling it's quite a story. Quite a story."

They discussed the whole thing during the evening. Leon came over on Sunday and they discussed it again. None of them could supply any answers, only questions.

But at least the discussions kept Heather from dwelling on what had happened between her and the stranger, something that she was grateful for. She didn't want to think about the stranger, and she was alarmed by the way his face kept popping into her mind. . . .

CHAPTER THREE

Heather overslept on Monday morning, largely because her thoughts had been so wrapped up in the painting and the stranger that she had forgotten to set her alarm the night before. Normally Lisa would have wakened her, but she wasn't planning to go to the office since she had worked on Saturday.

Frantically Heather dashed around the small apartment getting dressed. Silently she mouthed a half-rueful curse when she realized that the events of Saturday had driven such mundane matters as laundry from her mind. She had only one dress to wear. It was an unrelieved black with a high neckline and long sleeves, and though the thin wool clung to her slender body adoringly, black was still black, and she felt as if she should be on her way to a funeral.

After a hurried glance at the clock, Heather phoned for a cab and then quickly swept her long hair into a smooth chignon. With the final pin in place she surveyed her reflection in the dresser mirror wryly, deciding that if she was going to look severe, she might as well go all out. She failed to realize that the austere hairstyle and funereal dress only served to emphasize her delicate beauty and cool, remote manner.

She left the apartment quietly, locking the door behind her, and hurried down to find her cab waiting. She gave the driver the address of Norden and sat back with a breathless sigh. It irritated her to be late, not only because she was a punctual person, but because she liked to have the time to walk the few blocks to the office. It always started the day off badly if she found herself running late—not a good beginning on the day she would welcome a new boss.

Heather bit back a groan of protest as that thought presented itself, feeling too off-balance herself to cope with the little quirks and traits that would make up the unknown personality of her new agency head.

Norden had been the perfect employer, relying on her to keep his business affairs running on an even keel, but never intruding on her personal life. They had developed a friendly, casual relationship during the past two years, and Heather had gradually come to be more of an assistant than a secretary.

A perceptive man, Norden had quickly realized that Heather could handle any client, no matter how temperamental, and that she possessed an almost instinctive understanding of market trends. No matter what the product was, she seemed to know intuitively how best to advertise it, and Norden took full advantage of that talent. He had begun to ask her opinion about the various accounts and how they were being handled, to listen to her suggestions with real respect, and to encourage her to voice them without being asked.

Both Heather's suggestions and Norden's respect had increased over the months, with the result that Heather was now aware that she was, at least in part, responsible for the satisfaction of several of their most important clients. Her suggestions had prompted radical changes in several campaigns, changes that had widened the appeal of products and brought smiles to clients known for their hard-to-please attitudes. And since Norden was as appreciative as he was perceptive, her salary had risen somewhat dramatically.

Dramatically enough so that her new boss, unless Norden had taken him into his confidence, could easily be excused for wondering if she was perhaps more than a secretary.

As that thought occurred to her, Heather repressed an impulse to swear violently. It was hard enough to adjust to having a new boss, but the situation would become rapidly impossible if said boss had gained the mistaken impression that his secretary would be willing—not to say eager—to sit on his knee while taking dictation. Among other things.

Abruptly Heather recalled what Lisa had told her about Adam Blake, and her taut figure relaxed somewhat. If gossip was to be believed, it would seem that her new boss had sworn off women for the duration for whatever reason. Heather only hoped that the duration would endure for as long as she was Adam Blake's secretary.

It was not vain for Heather to suppose that Blake would find her attractive; she was going on past experience. Men always seemed to find her attractive, although she was a little puzzled as to their reasons. She knew that her figure was good; her artistic eye told her that her features were even and her eyes large and unusually brilliant. But Heather had never considered herself beautiful. And she had never understood why men watched her with strangely intent, probing eyes.

She would have been staggered to be told that the aloof manner she had cloaked herself in drew men like a magnet, that they were fascinated by the appearance of "still waters." She would not have understood that men were baffled and irritated by her passive submission to their instinctive dominance, unaware that even the most imperceptive of men could sense a stubborn resistance somewhere beneath the surface. Somewhere, at some deep level of her being, Heather had made a very quiet decision to allow no man dominion over her. It was that unconscious determination, striking a responsive cord at some animal-deep level of instinct, that drew men to her.

They saw a hauntingly beautiful woman, unconscious of her own beauty. They saw a delicate face carved from milk-white porcelain, cool to the touch and oddly unreal. She seemed fragile, defenseless, frail, breakable. And yet, in some manner, at some level they could only sense, she resisted. She made no attempt to assert herself, no attempt to impose her will on others. She submitted docilely to physical dominance, passive in a contest she knew to be unequal. And yet she resisted by the very act of her submission. She threw in her towel before the bell, conceded defeat before the battle.

And men looked into her brilliant violet eyes, conscious of an uncivilized, animal desire to shatter the porcelain mask she wore. They sensed somehow that there was nothing they could teach her of life, for there was no innocence in her eyes, only an oddly detached, other-world expression. And they wondered what she was beneath the still, beautiful face, wondered what it would take to reach her. They hungered to be the one to touch her, to reach down deep and find the part of herself she had locked away.

It is one of man's most ancient instincts—domination. He instinctively attempts to dominate, to possess, to own. His reach, as the poet observed, far exceeds his grasp. He must always strive for that which he cannot have, always stretch mightily for that which is just beyond reach. In the dim past it brought him out of the caves to look upon his world with possessive eyes; it began the age-old struggle with the female of his kind.

And it was that instinct, uncounted centuries deep, that stirred and came to life in the men who had wanted Heather. But she remained just beyond their grasp. However deeply they probed, however fiercely they attempted to impose their dominance, she was unreachable.

None of that was in Heather's mind as she paid her fare in front of Norden Advertising and hurried into the building. She was hoping that Lisa's gossip had been correct, that Adam Blake wanted nothing to do with women. It was never easy for a company like Norden to change ownership; too many clients were uneasy about drastic changes and were wary of new owners. She would need all her energy to deal with disturbed clients, not amorous employers.

The old scene in which a playboy boss chases his secretary around her desk had never seemed particularly funny to Heather.

She dashed down the hall as soon as the elevator had stopped on the top floor of the building and nodded abstractedly to familiar faces as she hurried past various offices filled with harried secretaries and even more harried executives. She could literally feel the unease of the entire building; everyone wondered what the new boss would be like. He knew advertising, but he didn't know *them*.

Reaching the end of the long hall, she opened the heavy paneled door, absently noting that Norden's brass nameplate had been removed, and went into her office. No one saw the owner of the company without first passing through her office, and she had gotten very good at putting off people her boss didn't want to see for one reason or another. Her office was empty, the connecting door to Norden's office closed, and she could faintly make out the rumble of male voices coming from inside.

Ignoring the sound, she sat down at her desk and put her purse into the bottom drawer, then opened the center drawer. Inside, she found a synopsis of the past week's events, left for her by the temporary who had taken her place. Reading the paper carefully, she picked up the phone and called the switchboard, telling the girl that she could take Norden's calls now. The buzzer sounded as she replaced the phone, and Heather immediately reached forward and touched the response key. "Yes, sir?"

"Come in here for a moment, please, Heather."

"Yes, sir." Heather's brows rose slightly, surprised that Norden had used her given name so casually with someone in his office. Then she realized that his "guest" was undoubtedly Adam Blake, and why should he keep up a pretense of formality around the man who was taking over the company? No reason at all. Except that it bothered her.

She pushed back her chair, rose, and went over to the connecting door, knocking lightly before entering. Norden came forward, smiling at her. He was a deceptively mild-looking man, with a cheerful smile and a portly build. People meeting him for the first time were often surprised at the impression he gave, surprised that such a mellow man could have built his impressive company from literally nothing.

Those who worked for him, however, were well aware of the almost-explosive energy and drive contained behind the smiling exterior. They knew him to be a shrewd, dynamic man who demanded the best effort from his employees and would be satisfied with nothing less. It was a measure of how well he was liked that none of his employees begrudged the extra effort he demanded.

"I'm sorry to be late, sir. I'm afraid I overslept."

"That's all right, Heather." Norden dismissed the apology with a wave of his hand. "I know how vacations are. I called you in here to meet your new boss. Lisa did tell you the news, didn't she?"

Heather smiled faintly and nodded, reflecting ruefully

that it was just like Norden to drop the bomb and then ask if she had been warned about it. "She told me."

"Good. Good. Well, I'll be taking him around to see the rest of the building and meet everyone, but I wanted you to be the first. You've been my right arm for the past two years, you know."

Touched, Heather murmured, "That's very kind of you, sir, but—"

"Nonsense! It isn't kind at all. It's the simple truth. I want Adam to know that he'll be getting a first-class assistant as well as a damned good secretary. You've been the power behind the throne, Heather, and don't try to deny it."

Her eyes widened slightly at the phrase and she almost winced. Desperately she hoped that it did not conjure up the same image in her new employer's mind that it provoked in her own. Power behind the throne, for God's sake.

Obviously unaware of having said anything out of place, Norden turned away from her slightly to indicate the man who had stood silently, out of her line of sight, by the desk. "Heather Richards, I want you to meet Adam Blake."

Heather looked toward her new boss, a faint, polite smile curving her lips. As the man stepped forward to greet her, the smile remained. Her delicate features didn't move by so much as a hair. But for a single, brief second, her violet eyes lost that peculiar other-world expression. She was horrified. She heard him speaking through the curious roaring in her ears.

"Miss Richards, I'm delighted to meet you. I've listened to James singing your praises all morning."

The voice was cool, the words faintly mocking, the expression in the black eyes impossible to read. Today he looked even more dangerous than she remembered, his physical strength evident beneath the impeccably tailored business suit. A leashed wolf. A caged tiger. A tethered hawk.

The stranger from the gallery.

Heather heard her own voice and was astonished at how normal it sounded. "Mr. Blake. I look forward to working with you." The words were conventional and sounded sincere. It convinced Norden.

But not Adam Blake. There was a gleam of mocking amusement in his black eyes, and Heather felt a sudden surge of pure rage. Damn him, he thought the whole thing was funny!

The phone rang before he could respond to her polite remark, and Norden went over to answer it. He uttered a few short phrases, then hung up and smiled apologetically at Blake. "There's a slight problem in the art department. If you'll excuse me for a few moments, I'll deal with it and leave you two to get acquainted."

Heather half-expected her new boss to demand to know what the problem was—it was now his company, after all—but he merely nodded and watched as the older man smiled encouragingly at Heather and left the room.

She wanted to demand angrily that he explain his behavior in the gallery, wanted to voice the impossible and confused suspicions rushing madly around in her mind, but she dared not utter a word.

For the first time she was consciously holding on to her remote screen, hiding behind it as if it were a battle shield. This man had touched her at some level she could not name, had somehow managed to rouse a physical response in her body. Even now, in spite of her furious anger, her body was responding to his maleness. She could feel her flesh warming, prickling in awareness, her heart thudding unevenly. Her lips burned as she helplessly remembered the heat of his kisses. Her loins ached at the memory of his hard body pressed against her.

Stop it! she ordered herself angrily, bitterly, knowing

that she was a fool for reacting so strongly to something that had probably struck him as being a particularly entertaining joke. He was watching her with that infuriating, amused smile, and she wanted to throw something at him.

Her cool expression didn't betray a thing, but her mind was working frantically. Instinct told her that she could not afford to lose her temper with this man, could not afford to let him slip beneath her guard as he had done at the gallery.

The human body possesses many instincts, just as the mind does, reacting in a moment of crisis or violent emotion. Heather's body reacted now with the instinct it shared with her mind—the instinct of self-preservation. This man could hurt her. Her body sensed its weakness next to his; her mind sensed her vulnerability placed alongside his confidence. She retreated further into herself than she had ever gone before, her senses dulling, her mind calming.

He was just a man. She looked at him with her violet eyes, seeing him only as her new boss, a stranger. She would not allow herself to see anything else. That aware, observant part of her mind, which could not be shut off, realized that he sensed the difference in her, was disturbed by it, but she ignored his recognition.

His black eyes narrowed, probing her face. "You look like a nun in that dress," he said finally. "Was it intentional? Did you intend to subdue your new boss?"

"No, sir," she replied calmly, politely, as though he had offered her a cup of coffee.

A flicker of anger showed briefly in his eyes. "No need to be so formal with me, sweet Heather," he drawled softly, seductively. "We've met before, remember?"

"I remember." Her voice was indifferent.

He stared at her for a long moment, and the intensity of his eyes would have frightened her if she had not hidden so thoroughly inside herself. He stepped forward, closer, invading the private territory that each human being claims and marks off. Heather neither flinched away nor tensed.

His gaze moved over her still face slowly, as if he were willing her to react to him, determined that she would. She met his eyes easily. After a long moment he murmured on a strange note of shock, "My God, you're hiding from me." His hand moved as though it were pulled by strings, jerking up, hesitating, gently touching her cheek. "What are you afraid of?"

Heather discovered that her senses were not as dull as she would have liked them to be. Her nerve endings tingled at the contact of flesh on flesh. She dismissed the sensation impatiently.

"Isn't it lonely in there?"

The question came softly, almost whispered, containing an odd thread of pain, of understanding. It was almost as if he, too, had suffered the anguish of unbearable loneliness, the torment of being locked inside himself.

And at that moment Heather knew that something had collapsed inside of her. With a painful rush everything seemed to come into focus. She could hear her heart beating, feel the blood surging through her veins. She stared at his face, her eyes registering her shock, bewildered, knowing now that she had no defense against this man. She was defenseless, utterly and totally. Vulnerable. Naked. And frightened.

Quite suddenly Heather felt an almost oppressive need to get away from Adam Blake. In some manner beyond her understanding, he had seen inside her sanctuary. His soft question had cut through all her barricades with the ease of a hot knife through butter, laying bare her very soul.

She tried to draw away from him, desperate to be alone and to try to understand what had just happened to her, but he wouldn't allow it. With a smothered sound he

56

pulled her against the hard length of his body, holding her in a comforting embrace. "I'm sorry," he whispered. "I know how scary it can be when the walls come tumbling down."

Heather remained rigid for a long moment, listening to his heart thud beneath her cheek. Then, with a sigh that seemed to come from somewhere deep inside her, she relaxed against him. She felt his arms tighten around her and tried to fight a sudden, absurd desire to burst into tears. "I don't understand," she murmured in the voice of a bewildered child seeking answers from someone it instinctively trusted.

"No," he mused softly, "I don't suppose you do." He rested his chin on the top of her head. "You've been hiding, sweet Heather, for a long time, I think. I just found you."

Aware that her body was, once again, responding to his nearness, Heather quickly pushed herself away from him, oddly disappointed when he released her without a struggle. "But, why *you*?" she asked desperately. "I don't even know you!"

He was smiling. "We can soon fix that."

She took another step backward, bitterly aware that she presented the appearance of a frightened mouse. "Look, Mr. Blake—"

"Adam," he interrupted.

"Mr. Blake," she continued firmly, "you're my employer, but nothing more! I'm not interested in—in anything else."

In a conversational tone he remarked, "It's a good thing I did away with that fortress of yours." When she looked blank, he smiled mockingly. "I think I've got a war on my hands," he explained, "and those walls were an unfair weapon."

Heather swallowed hard. "War?"

"Only a preliminary skirmish or two at this point, but

I feel sure it's going to be a war. You can't hide from me any longer, but you can still run, and we both know it."

Completely bewildered, Heather could only stare at him. "What are you talking about?"

He strolled casually over to the desk and sat on one corner, folding his arms across his broad chest and regarding her with a shatteringly charming smile. "What I'm talking about, sweet Heather, is our private little war. Just between you and me."

A feeling of foreboding crept over Heather at his words, but she forced herself to speak calmly. "I see. And just what is the objective of this war you've declared?"

"Getting you into my bed," he responded coolly.

Heather had a slight feeling that her mouth was hanging open. She had to try twice before her voice emerged. "That certainly isn't the most original proposition I've heard, but it is brief and to the point."

"I thought so." He sounded amused.

Heather struggled with herself for a moment, then succumbed to her anger. "You've got a hell of a nerve!"

He laughed softly. "You should get angry more often, Heather. You look almost human."

"If I only look human when I'm angry, I don't know why you want to bother with me," she retorted with icy emphasis.

"Stop fishing."

"I was not fishing!"

His black eyes gleamed. "No, but you certainly rise to the bait beautifully!"

Heather crossed her arms over her breasts in an obviously defensive gesture and glared at him. "Look. There is not going to be a war. Period. End of statement."

One slanted brow rose in mockery. "Are you waving a white flag already, sweet Heather? I thought you had more spirit."

She gritted her teeth in frustration. "Are you deaf? Or stupid? Or just plain out of your mind?"

"None of the above," he drawled. "It's quite simple, Heather. I heard the call to battle when I first saw you in that gallery. I expect resistance, of course, but I'll win in the end."

Fairly quivering with thinly leashed rage, Heather snapped, "Oh, you will, will you? You just crook your little finger and expect me to fall into bed with you?"

"I said that I expected resistance," he pointed out in the infuriating tone of one explaining something simple to a dimwitted child. "That's why it'll be a struggle. But you might as well wave that white flag now, because you're outgunned. On all sides."

Her violet eyes flashed with a look that should have cut him to ribbons. "Get it through your head, Mr. Blake: *I'm not interested!*"

"What? Without even fighting an opening engagement? Don't be silly, sweet Heather!" He was grinning openly. "I think I'm going to enjoy this."

Suddenly desperate to wipe out the seductive gleam in his black eyes, Heather exclaimed heatedly, "Mr. Blake, I consider your behavior most unbusinesslike."

Immediately he sobered. "During business hours we'll be polite and businesslike, nothing more. But outside these walls, the battle begins."

"Oh, I see," she said sarcastically. "It wouldn't do to set tongues wagging, would it? It's all right for you to try to seduce your secretary, but you don't want the knowledge to become public. Afraid it'll tarnish your image?"

A gleam of laughter lit the black eyes again. "Not at all."

"What happens if I spread the word?"

His smile remained. "You wouldn't do that," he said complacently. "You'll use fair weapons, just like I will.

You won't involve anyone else in our war, sweet Heather."

"Stop calling me that!" Her objection to his increasingly frequent form of address was as belated as it was feeble, and his widening grin proved that he realized that as well as she did. Hastily she added, "What makes you so sure I won't just resign and walk out of here?"

"You're not a coward," he responded softly, still smiling.

His determination was beginning to make her more nervous than angry. Abandoning reason, she said flatly, "You won't win."

"Of course I will, sweet Heather." His voice took on the same velvety blackness of his eyes, enticing, seductive. "I always win."

"I won't become your mistress!" What had made her say that? She was playing his game now.

He laughed softly, then spoke in a tone of absolute certainty. "To the victor go the spoils. I'm going to be your lover, Heather. Sooner or later. You might as well resign yourself."

"On a cold day in hell!"

He crossed the space between them in two long strides. Heather read the intention in his eyes as he reached out to grasp her shoulders, and her eyes widened in half-excited fear. "No! That's not fair," she objected, as though he had said something.

His head bent toward hers, the black eyes full of wicked amusement and something else. "You'll have to study up on tactics, sweet Heather, any good soldier knows the advancing army has the advantage of surprise."

She was trying desperately to hold him at bay, her small hands pushing at his broad chest. Breathlessly she exclaimed, "We're inside the office!"

"Sneak attack," he murmured, and his lips captured hers. He made no effort to be gentle. His lips parted hers

60

with a fiery demand that took her breath away. With the force of an actual physical shock, Heather felt the intrusion of his tongue, felt his hands slide down her back to pull her suddenly weak body against the strength of his. She was helpless to fight the surge of desire that threatened to consume her.

There was something almost desperate in his kiss, something raw and hungry, a painful yearning. It was as if he were starving for her, for the touch of her lips, for the feel of her slender body pressed against his own. His hands moved over her with unsteady eagerness, caressing, stroking, trying and failing to find satisfaction.

Heather's arms crept up around his neck, her mind nearly drowning in the waves of sensual pleasure sweeping over her. She felt one of his hands move slowly up her back to the smooth knot of hair at her nape, was vaguely aware of nimble fingers releasing the silky black mass from its severe style. It didn't matter.

She was back in the gallery, responding to a mysteriously fascinating stranger who had somehow cast a spell over her mind and body. This time, however, the emotions sweeping over her were even stronger than before. This man had snatched her from her fortress, pulling her out into the real world and making her helplessly aware of the demands of her body. Her mind screamed a warning, but it had little power, as it was in a shell quivering with hunger.

It was Adam who drew away at last, his arms still around her yielding body. "You see?" he murmured huskily. "This is one battle I'll always win."

She stared up at him, her eyes darkly purple, her mind only now regaining control over her traitorous body. Color swept up her throat and darkened her cheeks as his words—and her own realization—sank in. He *had* won. And his victory had been a full one, because she had not just submitted, she had responded.

She tore herself from his embrace with a violence that left nerve endings shrieking their unsatisfied demand. "One battle doesn't win a war!" she flung at him bitterly, the admission bringing a gleam to his eyes. "You won't win! I won't let you win!"

"I'll win." He caught her shoulders with hard fingers and gave her a little shake. "You *will* surrender to me!" The words were evenly spaced, harshly emphasized.

She was shaken by the wild glitter in his eyes, frightened, on a sheer animal level of instinct, by his fierce determination. He wanted to defeat her, dominate her, and that was something she could not allow. He had declared a war between them. Very well then, there would be a war. She'd fight him with every weapon she could find. She would *not* surrender!

For the first time, she voiced the stubborn determination that had been unconscious until now. Lifting her chin, she glared at him with a will as great as his own. "Don't be so sure of yourself, General!"

In her own office Heather collapsed in her chair and immediately reached for her compact. A glance in the mirror showed that her lips were slightly swollen and her lipstick was smeared. She looked as if she really had gone through a battle. Swearing silently, she quickly repaired her makeup and used the extra pins in her purse to put her hair back up.

When Norden came back a few minutes later, he found his ex-secretary as cool and collected as ever, except for the unexplained glitter in her eyes.

He paused by her desk, his glance keen. "Had a fight with the new boss already, Heather?"

His perception forced a surprised laugh from Heather. "Does it show so plainly?" she asked wryly.

His blue eyes twinkled slightly. "You look a little frayed around the edges. Was he throwing his weight around?"

"It was just a . . . clash of personalities, that's all."

"You've always been able to get along with anyone, Heather." Norden looked both amused and intrigued. "Blake must be an absolute monster if he was able to get a rise out of you!"

Heather thought of everything that had happened in the inner office, and her violet eyes became even more stormy. "Oh, we'll get it worked out," she said from between gritted teeth. "Even if it kills him."

It was Norden's turn to laugh in surprise. "That sounds serious! Want me to rake him over the coals?"

She shook her head with a rueful smile. "Never mind, James. We'll be too busy to worry about personalities, so it doesn't matter." She wished irritably that she believed her own words.

"Well, if you're sure." He smiled. "If my opinion counts for anything, I'd say you were equal to anything Blake could throw at you."

"Thanks," she murmured, hoping that he was right.

He gave her a conspiratorial wink, then went into the office which had been his own until today.

CHAPTER FOUR

Heather had to run the gamut of Alex's protective screens, waiting patiently each time she was told to hold on. The Sinclair Corporation was as vast as it was powerful; it wasn't possible to just call up Alex Sinclair unless you knew him very well. She was passed rapidly through the lower levels of the pyramid, amused when she realized that the people she talked to believed that she was the latest "playmate." She didn't bother to disabuse them, but simply kept telling them that she was a friend of Mr. Sinclair's and needed to talk to him.

At long last she reached his private secretary and was put through to Alex with surprising speed—something that made Heather suspect that he was hoping for a call from Lisa.

"Sinclair." His voice was as cool and well-bred as she remembered.

"Alex, this is Heather Richards. I don't know if you remember me, but—"

"Of course I remember you, Heather." His voice had relaxed somewhat, deepened in amusement. "You're not the kind of woman a man easily forgets." He hesitated, then went on quickly, "There's nothing wrong, is there? Lisa?"

The anxiety in his voice made Heather surer than ever that she was doing the right thing. "No, Lisa's fine," she reassured him quickly. "I just need to talk to you, Alex. Do you think—are you free for lunch today?"

There was a short pause, and then he said quietly, "What time shall I pick you up?"

Heather sighed in relief. "Would noon be all right?"

"Fine." Rather dryly, he went on, "I don't know what you have in mind, Heather, but I get the feeling that this discussion should take place in private. Would my penthouse fit the bill?"

Well aware that she had nothing to fear from Alex, Heather laughed softly. "If you have a good cook."

"A very good cook. Shall I pick you up at the office?"

Knowing that he would come inside the office in the hope of seeing Lisa, Heather said immediately, "That'll be fine. I'll see you at noon then."

"Noon it is."

Heather hung up the phone and sat back with a satisfied smile. She couldn't have planned it better. If Adam was there when Alex came up . . . War, huh? She'd show him war!

She worked steadily throughout the morning. A little before twelve, she prepared for her lunch date, redoing her makeup and deliberately letting down her hair. Surveying the results, she was satisfied.

The loose hairstyle gave her face a softened look, and her careful makeup emphasized it. She stared into the mirror for a moment, then grimaced slightly, reminding herself silently that she had decided to use every weapon she could find. Something told her, however, that this particular weapon could be a dangerous one.

She steeled herself against a sudden quiver of uncertainty and put the compact away in her purse. There was nothing wrong with what she was doing, after all. Her lunch date with Alex was perfectly innocent. Of course, she didn't intend to tell Adam that.

The phone rang just then, and she picked it up. It was the guard downstairs, asking permission for Alex Sinclair to come up. Pleased that she had read his intentions correctly, Heather told the guard to send him up.

She had just pulled her purse out of her desk drawer when the door opened and Adam came in. His eyes immediately narrowed as he took in her changed appearance. "Going somewhere?"

Heather looked pointedly at the clock on the wall and then back at Adam. "To lunch. It is that time, you know."

He lounged against one of the filing cabinets, his smile mocking. "Where were you planning on going?"

"I'll leave that up to my date." She sat back and regarded him with cool eyes. "He should be here any moment now."

Adam's smile vanished. A dangerous gleam entered his eyes. "You're going out with me, Heather." His voice was the soft growl of a lion on the prowl.

"I don't remember being asked." She continued to stare at him with unreadable eyes. "In any case, I'm afraid that I'm all booked up for quite some time. Sorry about that."

"Don't play with me, Heather," he warned softly.

"Play?" She looked sweetly bewildered. "I don't know what you're talking about."

"You know." There was a suggestion of leashed violence in him, a brooding anger that was as deadly as it was unexpected. "Is this your strategy, Heather, using other men to get to me?"

A part of Heather wished suddenly that she had not started this; his attitude was like the quiet before the storm. But she held on to her courage with both hands and smiled at him with spurious innocence. "Does it get to you?" she asked softly.

His face tightened. "You learn fast," he grated, without answering her question. Or perhaps that was an answer.

"I'm a quick study," she said lightly, and rose to her feet with silent gratitude when the outer door opened.

Alexander Sinclair stepped into the room and Heather was immediately aware of an atmosphere of almost lethal hostility. The two men were much the same height and build; they both walked and moved with grace. Both wore an air of command, as though expecting their slightest order to be obeyed instantly. All similarities ended there.

Alex was fair where Adam was dark, with silver-blond hair and brilliant emerald eyes. He looked ten years younger than the thirty-nine Heather knew him to be, lean and fit from years of hard work and even harder play. He was a man who smiled more often than he frowned, laughed more often than he raged.

He was smiling when he came into the room, but that smile disappeared when he saw Adam. He inclined his head slightly. "Adam." When Adam only nodded rather abruptly, Alex went on in a slightly strained voice. "I heard that you were taking over Norden, but I hadn't realized that it would be this soon."

Again, Adam only nodded. With an odd sigh Alex turned his eyes to Heather. "Ready, Heather?"

Tearing her eyes from the face that looked as though it had been carved in granite, Heather looked at her escort. "Yes, yes, I'm ready." She went around the desk and crossed to Alex's side. Without looking at Adam she murmured, "I'll be back in an hour."

"See that you are." His voice was silky.

They went out of the office, and as Alex started to close the door behind them, Heather glanced back involuntarily. Her gaze met Adam's for a brief second, and she felt an icy coldness seep into her body. Something terrible was happening in his eyes.

That look stayed with Heather all the way to Alex's

penthouse. She hardly noticed the hand at her elbow as they made their way from the building, was barely aware of being seated in the passenger side of a racy-looking foreign sportscar. She never saw the concerned, puzzled glances that Alex was throwing her from time to time. Only one thought filled her mind.

For some inexplicable reason Alex Sinclair was the last man in the world she should have flaunted beneath Adam's nose.

Adam hadn't been angry merely because she had chosen to flaunt another man in front of him; she was certain of that. Oh, he had been angry, but his anger had increased tenfold when Alex had walked into the room. The two men had faced each other with all the cordiality of stray tomcats. And Heather sensed that the hostility was mainly on Adam's part. Alex had simply been guarded, as a man would be when faced with someone who strongly disliked him.

Strong dislike? That was far too mild a term for the emotions she had felt radiating from Adam.

She looked up suddenly, realizing that they were in an underground garage. Alex parked the car and then came around to open her door. "Are you back now?" he asked gently.

Heather climbed out of the car rather hastily. "Back?"

Alex closed the door, then took her arm and began leading her toward the elevator. "I don't know where you were," he said dryly, "but you weren't with me."

"Oh." She felt a flush creeping up her cheeks. "Sorry. I was thinking."

"I see." He flicked an oblique glance at her as they entered the elevator. "Known Adam long?" he asked as he pressed the button for the penthouse.

It sounded as if he were changing the subject; Heather knew that he wasn't. "No," she answered calmly, biting back an impulse to ask him the same question.

"Odd." Alex stared fixedly at the elevator doors. "He seemed very possessive about you."

So he had seen the killing look Adam had given him as they had turned to leave. "I can't imagine why," she murmured lightly.

Alex looked down at her for a moment and then fell silent. Either the subject held no interest for him, or else he realized that Heather didn't want to talk about it. She had a feeling that it was the latter, and she was grateful.

A few moments later they were entering the subdued luxury of Alex's penthouse. It was decorated tastefully but, unlike most of its kind, bore a lived-in appearance. Magazines were strewn across the coffee table in the living room, pillows were piled on the carpet by the stereo system, two tennis rackets reposed on a chair, houseplants of every kind abounded.

Heather smiled as she noticed the plants—a passion of Lisa's—and then went over to pick up a silver-framed photograph of Lisa sitting on a side table. Alex had excused himself and left the room, and as soon as he returned, she said, "This is good. How did you get her to pose for it?"

Alex grimaced slightly. "It wasn't easy, believe me. Why is she so rabid on the subject of being photographed? She is a photographer, after all."

"That's why." Heather put the picture down and turned to him with a smile. "Every time she shows up somewhere with her cameras, someone always says that she should be a model. It irritates her."

He laughed. "So that's it. I always wondered." With a gesture toward the hall, he said, "Honey has lunch ready." As Heather's eyes widened in astonishment, he held up a defensive hand and laughed again. "It's her name, I swear! She's my housekeeper."

Smiling, Heather followed him into the dining room,

reflecting that it must have been Alex's laugh that had caused Lisa to fall in love with him.

Honey turned out to be middle-aged, five feet tall, five feet wide, and every bit as cheerful as she looked. She slapped plates before them with a fine disregard for the expensive china and contributed to the conversation with an air of having said the final word on the subject. She bullied Alex as though he were her son, advised Heather on the subject of men in general and rich ones in particular, and generally made private conversation between Heather and Alex impossible.

Heather was hard-put to keep from laughing, but she was beginning to feel a little desperate by the time the meal was concluding. Then Alex literally pleaded with Honey to leave them alone, and he did it so outrageously that the housekeeper left the room laughing.

As the door swung shut behind her, Alex turned to Heather with a laugh. "She's a fantastic housekeeper and cook, but . . ."

Heather lowered the napkin she had been using to hide her wide smile, her violet eyes shining with amusement. "Does she always act like that?"

"Always." Alex grinned slightly, then sobered. "You only have about ten minutes left of your lunch hour."

Her own laughter fading, Heather looked down at her plate for a moment and then met his eyes levelly. "Lisa's my best friend, and I don't want to see her get hurt. That's why I wanted to talk to you. I'm going to ask an impertinent question; I only hope that you understand it's justified." She waited for his slow nod and then asked flatly, "Are you in love with Lisa?"

For a moment she thought he was going to deny it, and then he seemed to slump slightly. He pushed his plate away with a faint grimace of distaste and sat back in his chair. "So much so that I've been going quietly out of my

70

...nd these past weeks," he told her tiredly, his emerald eyes suddenly dark with pain.

Heather pushed her own plate away. "Then why don't you do something about it?" she chided gently.

He laughed shortly. "What would you have me do—knock her over the head and drag her off somewhere?" His voice was bitter. "I did everything but go down on my knees to her, and she acted as if I'd insulted her."

Heather tried to think of a tactful way of explaining the situation to him and finally settled for honesty. "Think about it for a minute, Alex. With your reputation and the fact that you've avoided matrimony like the plague for nearly twenty years, Lisa was afraid to take you seriously. She wanted to, but—"

"Wanted to?" Alex's head snapped up.

"She's miserable," Heather murmured with a smile.

He frowned slightly. "So it was my reputation that bothered her all along?" When Heather nodded, he exclaimed impatiently, "Hell, my reputation is all a lot of hot air! I thought Lisa realized that."

Heather shrugged slightly. "I guess Lisa figured that where there was smoke, there was bound to be a fire. And people have been telling her for weeks about the different women you've been seeing. Weekend guests, expensive gifts, and the like."

Alex looked bewildered. "*What* different women? The only woman I've taken out since Lisa stopped seeing me was Teri Evans, and that was more or less from habit."

"From habit?" Heather gazed at him searchingly.

"Sure. Teri fell apart when her husband, who happened to be my best friend, was killed ten years ago, and she sort of leaned on me." He shrugged. "She'll be announcing her engagement next week. Some guy she met in New York—a stockbroker, I think."

"Everyone thinks that she's in love with you."

"Everyone?" His puzzled frown turned suddenly into a

71

look of understanding. "Lisa thought so too?" When Heather nodded, he sighed quietly. "There's nothing between Teri and me, Heather, not even a kiss. She's in love with this broker of hers, and I'm so besotted over Lisa that nothing else matters. I've been working twelve hours a day ever since she more or less told me to go to hell in a bucket. I don't know where she heard those rumors, but there's nothing to them."

"Nothing?"

"Nothing," he confirmed flatly. "Oh, I can't deny that I earned my reputation years ago. I'm thirty-nine, and there have been women in my life; I'm a perfectly normal man. But I don't have a harem, as one gossip column maintained, and the road behind me isn't littered with broken hearts."

With a rueful shrug he muttered, "If I'm seen twice in public with the same woman, the press proclaims that she's my latest mistress. And no one bothers to ask either me or the lady involved."

Heather smiled faintly. "Hot air?"

Alex grimaced. "For the most part. I've dated a lot of women, but only because I was looking, like most men, I think, for that special one." He laughed mirthlessly. "And when I finally find that special one and get up the nerve to propose to her, she tells me to get lost!"

With a rueful look Heather said, "There's no way I can explain why Lisa reacted the way she did. You'll have to ask her yourself."

He looked uncertain. "Will she see me?"

"Why don't you surprise her?" Heather rose with a smile. "She's at home today." She glanced at her watch and then gave an impatient exclamation. "And I'm going to be late! Can you spare the time to drop me at the office, or should I call a cab?" She eyed him teasingly.

He laughed and, rising, came around the table to her side. "I think I can spare the time!"

Ten minutes later Alex pulled his sportscar into a no-parking zone in front of Norden. Heather stopped him with a lifted hand when he started to get out and said, "Don't bother. I know how anxious you are to see Lisa." Her violet eyes sparkled with sudden amusement. "And you darned well better get everything straightened out between you, otherwise Lisa will kill me for interfering!"

He chuckled softly, and then half-turned in the seat to give her a grave smile. "Thank you, Heather," he said quietly.

She leaned forward suddenly, impulsively, to kiss him lightly on the cheek. "Good luck!" And she slid quickly from the car.

As she started toward the building, he called out, "We'll name our first child Heather!"

Over her shoulder she retorted laughingly, "Better hope the poor kid's a girl then!" and went into the building, still laughing, as the roar of Alex's sportscar died away.

She got into the elevator and rode up to her floor with a small, amused smile, wondering what Lisa would do when she opened the door to find Alex. Moments later she was back at her desk. She had just started to reach for the phone to notify the switchboard that she had returned when the outer door opened and Adam stormed into the room, his handsome face still retaining that granite-hewn look of primitive savagery.

"You're late," he bit out.

Heather stared at him in astonishment as he stood in front of her desk, and for a moment wondered if he could possibly be so angry because she was a few minutes late. As coolly as she could manage, she said, "I'm sorry. It won't happen again." She deliberately didn't explain *why* she was late.

He took a step toward her, and Heather could literally feel his fury. "What is there between you and Alex Sin-

73

clair?" he jerked out, as if the question were torn from him.

"That's none of your business," she 'replied calmly, turning on her typewriter and efficiently inserting a sheet of paper.

Adam leaned across the desk and ripped the paper from the machine in a violent gesture that took Heather completely by surprise. "Damn you, I'm *making* it my business! And it will be *everybody's* business soon, I have no doubt! Sinclair has quite a track record where women are concerned. Is he your lover?"

The question shocked Heather oddly. "That, too, is none of your business," she answered, only just managing to hide her own rising anger.

"Why did you go to his penthouse?"

That question brought her to her feet in mingled surprise and wrath. "How do you know where we went?" she demanded furiously.

"I followed you. How the hell do you think I know?"

"You *followed* us?" Her violet eyes were stormy. "You had no right! Where I go and what I do on my own time is no one's business but my own, and I'll thank you to remember that!"

In two long strides he came around the desk to grasp her shoulders across the typewriter. "I have every right, damn you! You went with him just to get to me!" he gritted. "Do you think I don't know that?"

Dizzy from the shaking, thoroughly enraged now, Heather said breathlessly, "I wasn't aware this 'combat' of yours extended to physical violence."

His hands fell away from her abruptly; he stepped back as though she had struck him. "I'm sorry," he said contritely. "I didn't mean to touch you." Then again his mood suddenly changed as he raised his hand in a gesture of supplication. "God, Heather, tell me you didn't sleep with that man!"

74

Heather stood, stunned, mystified. Was he serious? Was that a tremor she'd heard in his voice?

Suddenly the outer door opened and Norden entered. "Heather, is—oh, there you are, Adam. The meeting's ready to roll. Are you—" Norden stepped inside, his voice breaking off abruptly as he became aware of the silent tension of the room. "Is something wrong?"

Heather had turned slightly as the door opened. She could not have answered Norden if her life had depended on it.

Adam's hand fell to his side; his expression smoothed out. He started toward the door, saying calmly, "No, nothing's wrong. Let's get the meeting started. We have a lot of ground to cover."

Heather stood silent, her face averted, until the door closed behind them. Then she sank limply into her chair. God, what was wrong with her? She toyed with the bracelet on her wrist, staring across the room with disturbed eyes.

Why had she been dimly conscious of a twisted desire to hurt Adam, to see him flinch? And why did she feel anything at all toward him? She had met—no, encountered—him for the first time only two days before. They were virtual strangers.

Almost immediately her mind amended the thought. No. They were not strangers. There *was* something between them, although she was at a loss to define it. Is that what he had meant by having a right to her? Some unspoken right of possession? Physical attraction? Oh, yes, quite definitely. But it wasn't only that. He seemed to have the power to rouse violent emotions within her, just as she could do with him.

Disturbed by the thought, Heather hastily began her afternoon work. She didn't want to examine her feelings too closely. Not right now. The examination might weaken her certainty regarding her ability to resist Adam

Blake, and that was something she didn't need. Uncertainty could easily be her downfall.

Heather worked steadily throughout the afternoon, barely glancing up when Adam and Norden went through to the inner office. They were in and out during the remainder of the day as Norden briefed Adam on clients and accounts and the other things he would have to know to assume control of the company. Heather answered the telephone, spoke soothingly to worried clients, and occasionally carried files or reports into the inner office as they were requested.

During those times she neither looked at Adam nor spoke to him. But she could feel him looking at her. And she was aware of the fury seething just beneath his surface calm. The battle that she had launched with her lunch date had not ended, she knew. It was a temporary cease-fire, that was all.

The two men were out of the office at five, and Heather hastily finished up her work and left, hoping to avoid Adam. She felt like a coward as she hurried down the hall to the elevator, but consoled herself with the thought that even the most courageous of armies sometimes retreated in the face of the enemy when circumstances were against them. She smothered a giggle as she walked past the guard's desk in the lobby and waved to him, wondering wryly if she would spend the rest of her life thinking in military terms.

Of all the absurdities! Fancifully she wondered if she could apply to the government for military aid, the thought bringing a smile to her face. The smile died abruptly as she emerged onto the sidewalk.

A gleaming silver-gray Mercedes was parked in front of the building, low-slung and powerful. Adam leaned casually against the fender, coat discarded, tie loosened. The light spring breeze blew his black hair into attractive disarray, giving him a rakish appearance.

As Heather stopped short, he said tersely, "Get in." His voice was cool, his black eyes unreadable. He straightened lazily, like a great jungle cat, smooth power in the movement.

Heather gave him a go-to-hell look, belied by the nervous tremor in her lower lip, and started to turn to take her usual route home.

In one easy stride he had reached her side and gripped her wrist with steely insistence. "Would you like me to put you in?" he asked casually.

Heather stared up at him. He was smiling. She glanced around, seeing departing Norden employees casting furtive, curious looks at the two still figures. What was that about discretion being the better part of valor? With a mental shrug of defeat, she turned toward the car.

She made no attempt to escape when Adam closed her door and went around to the driver's side of the car. As he started the powerful machine with a roar and pulled out into the stream of traffic, she opened her mouth to tell him where she lived, but he forestalled her.

"I know where you live," he told her flatly. His hands gripped the steering wheel, his knuckles white with tension, his eyes fixed on the road ahead.

Heather discovered that her gaze was riveted on his long-fingered hands, a peculiar pulse pounding in her throat as she stared at them. A tiny part of her mind noted almost idly that he could easily strangle her with those powerful hands, and immediately she tore her eyes away to stare straight ahead.

With a start of surprise she realized that Adam was parking the car in the lot beside her apartment building, and she reached quickly for the door handle. "Thanks for the lift—"

"Not just yet," he growled, grasping her wrist and pulling her around on the seat so that they faced each other across the gear console. "You have a question to answer."

Heather tried to pull her hand away, then gave up the attempt when he retained his hold with the easy strength which would, she knew, always defeat her. "I don't know what you're talking about," she said.

His fingers tightened almost painfully on her wrist. "You know. I want a simple answer, yes or no. Is Alex Sinclair your lover?"

She stared into the obsidian pools of his eyes, her own eyes stormy with the anger he always seemed to provoke. It wiped away her nervousness. It made her reckless. "I've already given you all the answers I'm going to."

Suddenly he yanked her toward him, his black eyes flaring with a savage emotion she could not comprehend. She was crushed against his body from the waist up, the gear console preventing more intimate contact. His lips came down on hers with brutal force, the punishing onslaught shocking her into immobility. His mouth ground against hers, cruel, untamed, filled with sheer, unmitigated rage.

Shock yielded to anger. Heather began to struggle against him, fiercely pushing at his chest and shoulders. She might as well have attempted to buckle the Golden Gate bridge. Twisting and turning, she at last managed to tear her lips from his. "Let go of me!"

Steely fingers grasped a handful of hair to hold her head steady. And then his mouth was once again crushing hers in a kiss meant to degrade, to humiliate.

For the first time, his kisses stirred no desire in Heather. She continued to struggle in his cruel embrace, angrily gritting her teeth against him, refusing to respond.

Finally he released her, his chest heaving, a flickering wildness in his eyes. "Get out," he said harshly, "before I . . . Just go, damn you." His voice had a raw, aching sound.

Angry and hurt, Heather didn't take the time to answer him. She opened the car door and tumbled out, slamming

78

it behind her and rushing into the building as if all the demons in hell were after her. She got as far as the stairs before she was forced to stop, out of breath, and lean against the railing. It was then that she realized she had left her purse in Adam's car. Involuntarily she glanced back through the glass doors: the Mercedes was gone.

She stared out for a long moment, then turned to slowly climb the stairs, vaguely hoping that Lisa was at home. Otherwise she'd have to get the manager to let her in. Outside the apartment door she tried to restore her hair to some kind of order, painfully remembering Adam's fingers raking through it. Pushing the memory away, she tried the doorknob. It was unlocked. With a sigh of relief she went inside and closed the door.

She took only two steps before realizing Lisa wasn't alone. They were cuddled together on the couch, their faces wearing twin expressions of blissful happiness, and Heather felt like an interloper. "I'm sorry," she apologized quickly as they rose to their feet. She looked wryly at Alex. "I thought you'd be gone by now."

He grinned as he turned toward her. "We had a lot to straighten out." Then his grin faded.

At the same moment Lisa said worriedly, "Heather, your mouth's bleeding! What happened?"

Automatically Heather raised a hand to her mouth. She wiped away the drop of blood and stared at her fingers for a few seconds. "I must have bit my lip," she said lightly.

Quietly Alex said, "It looks as if you've been hit in the mouth." His eyes searched her pale features narrowly.

"Don't let looks deceive you," Heather said calmly as she came into the room. "Lisa, is that a diamond I see?"

Her friend accepted the change of subject, at least for the moment. "Do you like it?" Almost shyly she held out her left hand, the third finger graced with a lovely pear-shaped diamond.

"It's beautiful," Heather responded honestly. She

79

looked at Alex in amusement. "How long have you been carrying this around?"

"I bought it the day after I met Lisa, as I have just spent some hours convincing her, and I've carried it ever since."

Heather smiled, then turned her gaze to her friend. "Have you told your father yet?" she asked.

It was Alex who answered. "About an hour ago." He grimaced slightly. "I don't flatter myself that he was pleased. I am only nine years younger than he is, after all."

"Will you *stop* with the age thing?" Lisa demanded, frowning at him fiercely. "I happen to love you just the way you are!"

He took an involuntary step toward her, his emerald eyes glowing, and Heather hastily held up a hand. "Hold it a second. Don't go into another huddle just yet!" She smiled teasingly at Lisa's red face, then looked at Alex. "There's something I want to ask you."

Reluctantly Alex tore his gaze from the face of his wife-to-be. "What is it?"

Heather hesitated, then asked flatly, "Why does Adam Blake hate you so much?"

CHAPTER FIVE

"I honestly don't know," Alex grimaced slightly. "I've met Adam from time to time over the years. He's always been a bit—disapproving"—his emerald eyes probed Heather's unreadable expression—"but never as hostile as he was today."

"Today?" Lisa frowned. "Oh, you mean when you went to the office to pick Heather up?" She looked at her friend with sudden suspicion. "Heather, when did you meet Adam Blake?"

"We were introduced this morning," Heather murmured, stretching a point slightly.

Alex and Lisa exchanged looks. Alex shrugged slightly and murmured, "If a look could kill, I wouldn't be here right now."

Lisa apparently had no trouble understanding this cryptic remark. She stared at Heather. "Does Adam Blake fancy you, Heather?" When her friend avoided her eyes, she murmured, "They said he wasn't interested in women."

"*They said!*" Heather exclaimed bitterly. "The most inaccurate phrase in the English language!" She flushed suddenly as two pairs of bright, inquiring eyes fastened onto her.

"Then he *does* fancy you!" Lisa sounded amused.

Heather gave her an irritated look. "Do you have to use that word? *Fancy,* for God's sake! It makes me sound like—like—"

"Never mind what it makes you sound like," Lisa dismissed impatiently. "Is it true?"

"I've only just met the man," Heather responded, trying to infuse her voice with outrage, and succeeding only in sounding defensive.

Lisa ignored the defense. "Well, well," she murmured. "Daddy had better watch out if Adam Blake's in there pitching; that is, if he's everything he's described as being. Is he, Heather?"

"I suppose he's quite handsome," Heather said in an offhand voice, resolutely avoiding her friend's too-perceptive eyes. "His personality is another thing entirely."

"His personality? You mean you've actually found someone you can't get along with?"

The incredulous question caught Heather off guard. Without stopping to think, she replied heatedly, "Adam Blake is as easy to get along with as a hungry lion!"

Inexplicably Lisa started laughing. Even Alex looked amused, and Heather glared at the both of them. Stiffly she said, "I don't find anything even remotely funny in the fact that I've just compared my employer to a predatory animal."

"Oh, Heather, you don't know just how funny it is!" Lisa said unsteadily, wiping her streaming eyes. "Adam Blake must be part . . . sorcerer."

It was clear that Heather still failed to find the humor in the situation. "You're talking in riddles," she snapped.

Sobering, Lisa gazed at her friend with wry eyes. "Heather, ever since I've known you, you've been away somewhere."

Knowing that Lisa was right, Heather stared down at the bracelet on her wrist. "Since the accident," she murmured. "But what has that got to do with Adam Blake?"

"I think you know." Lisa smiled slightly. "You've been changing ever since you saw that portrait, Heather. But today—today, you're like a different person. And if Adam Blake's done that to you, then all I can say is that he has my vote!"

"You don't know what you're saying." Heather started to giggle suddenly as the humor of Lisa's remark struck her. "You're throwing me to the lion, friend. Condemning me to a fate worse than death."

Lisa grinned. "Oh, I have faith in you, friend. You're part witch yourself. Adam Blake better look to his defenses!"

Heather stared at her friend with such a peculiar expression that Alex and Lisa exchanged baffled looks. Finally, in a carefully expressionless voice, Heather said, "Yes, indeed. Adam Blake had better look to his defenses." She realized abruptly that they were staring at her as though she had taken leave of her senses, and she laughed suddenly. "I haven't gone off the deep end," she assured them cheerfully. "As a matter of fact I feel normal for the first time today. And I am going to take a nice long hot bath and build up a few defenses of my own. Why don't you two go out and celebrate?"

Still eyeing her a bit uncertainly, Alex said, "We were planning to, but we wanted you to come along. If it hadn't been for you—"

"Count me out," Heather interrupted firmly. "Engaged couples should always celebrate alone. That way no one else can be embarrassed by passionate glances across the table." She watched in amusement as the two exchanged just such a glance.

Half an hour later Heather was alone in the apartment. She filled the tub with hot water, adding bubble bath with a generous hand. It felt marvelous to relax in the steaming, scented water, and Heather could feel the tension ease away.

She was beginning to take an extremely light-hearted view of her war with Adam Blake, and she occupied her mind in the bath by composing a letter of protest to the government. *Some maniac has declared war on a peaceful citizen of a peaceful country. Someone should do something about him. Put him in irons. Keelhaul him. Send him to the guillotine in a tumbrel. Something.*

It was a game, that's all. Just a game. Heather conveniently forgot the overwhelming emotions of the day. It was a game.

She should have considered Russian roulette—that was a game. A deadly game. She should have remembered that children who played with matches thought of their pastime as a game. . . .

The shrill ring of the telephone interrupted Heather's thoughts. Mildly irritated, she climbed from the tub and glanced around for a towel. No towel. Damn. Barefoot and dripping, she padded into the bedroom and lifted the receiver. Lightly she said, "Hello?"

"Heather?"

She decided absently that the room was chilly. "Oh, hello, General. You can't conduct battles over the telephone, you know. The telephone company wouldn't like it. They frown on obscene calls." There was a long silence, and Heather was vaguely pleased to realize that the gentleman on the other end of the line was somewhat taken aback by her insouciant remarks. *That's one for our side!* she thought cheerfully.

"Have you been drinking?" he demanded at last.

"Not at all," she told him airily. "As a matter of fact I was taking a bath. And this room's drafty. So, if you wouldn't mind—"

"What are you wearing?" he asked abruptly, cutting her off.

Heather stared down at herself. "Afraid I'm out of uniform, General," she responded lightly. "I'm wearing a thin, a very thin—layer of dissolving bubbles."

Her remark was answered by utter silence.

"Is something wrong, General? Your gun backfire? Your trusty charger fall and break a leg?"

"No." He was beginning to sound slightly amused. "But the thought of you standing there talking to me wearing nothing but bubbles is driving me out of my mind!"

"Just don't ask me to dance with fans," she told him sweetly and hung up. She made it halfway across the room before the phone started ringing again. With a sigh she returned to it and picked up the receiver.

"Damn it, don't hang up on me!" he told her without preamble.

"Look, do you mind if we continue this extremely pointless discussion another time?" she responded tranquilly. "My bubbles are fast disappearing, and—"

He groaned. "What are you trying to do to me, Heather?"

"I wasn't aware that I was trying to do anything."

"You know damn well what you're doing," he insisted huskily. "I get tied up in knots just looking at you with your clothes on. I'm going crazy imagining you wearing only a smile."

"Then don't imagine it," she advised him kindly. "Besides, I'm not smiling. I'm shivering. And I'd like to finish my bath. See you on the battlefield, General."

The third time, Heather ignored the phone's shrill demand. Several minutes later the ringing finally ceased, only to start up again almost immediately. Still Heather ignored it. Emerging once again from the now-tepid bath, she drained the tub with a faint sigh, then dried herself with a thick, fluffy towel. By the time she had donned her zip-up, floor-length robe, the ringing had stopped.

She took down her hair, which she had pinned up for her bath, and sat at her dressing table to brush it. The strokes became slower and slower, finally halting altogether. Heather put the brush down on the table and stared into the reflection of her violet eyes, suddenly realizing that her light-hearted mood had vanished as abruptly as it had come. She felt tired, drained. And not a little bewildered. There was nothing funny in her situation, nothing funny at all.

The events of the day washed over her with sudden force, unclouded by emotion, unaffected by Adam Blake's mocking presence. Like a movie run in slow motion, she saw the whole day happening again, heard every word. His uncanny insight of the morning, his cool declaration of war, his possessive attitude, his seething rage when she had gone out to lunch with Alex, the brutal embrace in his car—none of it made any sense.

Unless she accepted the explanation that Adam himself had offered: he wanted her. *Wanted* her. For some inexplicable reason, he had decided that he was going to become her lover. Or was it inexplicable? Quite suddenly she remembered his statement in the gallery: *That's a challenge no red-blooded man could ignore. I thought I'd have a shot at it.*

Was that it? God, did he want her only because her reputation proclaimed that no man could arouse a response in her? Was he determined to prove his manhood by thawing the Ice Princess?

But he had already. Heather shied away from the admission, then faced it squarely. He had thawed the ice. He, a total stranger, had roused a response in her that no other man had even come close to. And he knew it. Then why did he. . .

The question faded into nothingness as its answer

86

popped, unbidden, into Heather's mind. He wanted it all. He wanted her to surrender to him totally, completely.

Her mind's eye saw his black eyes glint with determination, his lean body move with powerful, catlike grace, and she shivered suddenly. How could she fight him when her body felt the pull of his attraction with every nerve it possessed? What weapons could she use against him? She couldn't use another man as a buffer between them. Aside from Adam's violent reaction to her "gesture" of today, she simply couldn't use a man like that.

The only weapon she had was her stubborn determination to resist him. It seemed, quite suddenly, a puny defense against his iron-willed determination.

Her thoughts were interrupted by the doorbell ringing. Heather rose from the dressing table with a weary sigh. She moved through the apartment, absently wondering if perhaps Leon had come over to discuss his daughter's engagement. She opened the door, her smile of welcome dying on her lips.

Adam Blake lounged against the doorjamb, holding Heather's purse in one powerful hand. "I came to return lost property." His dark, hooded gaze swept the length of her body, taking in the deep purple robe which made her eyes appear more brilliant.

She held out a hand. "Thank you," she responded distantly. "I'll see you tomorrow in the office, no doubt."

"No doubt," he agreed blandly, stepping past her calmly and walking into the living room. "Unless I get run over by a truck or something." An oddly charming smile spread across his face when he turned to see her still standing by the door. "That was what you were hoping, wasn't it? That I'd get run over by a truck?"

"The thought did occur to me," she snapped, slamming the door and following him into the room. "Look, I appreciate your bringing the purse over, but I wish you'd leave. I'm not dressed for company."

"But you are dressed," he drawled softly. "Pity. I was looking forward to seeing you in the bubbles."

Heather felt hot color sweep up her cheeks. Now she regretted her breezy phone conversation with this dangerous man. Torn between embarrassment at her unintentionally provocative remarks and anger over his uninvited presence in her home, she settled on anger. "I'm getting fed up with your little games, Mr. Blake!"

He stepped toward her suddenly, his face serious—deadly serious. "It's no game, sweet Heather," he told her softly. "I issued a challenge today, and you accepted it. No, more than that, you issued a challenge of your own. There's no going back for either of us."

Heather felt a peculiar chill as she listened to his words, a sensation of having suddenly lost control of the situation. She had to swallow hard before finding her voice. And her voice was small and treacherously unsteady. "I can't take another day like today." It was an admission she hated making, but it had to be made.

For a moment his face gentled, but then it hardened again. "I won't apologize for my behavior, Heather," he said harshly, dropping her purse on the couch and staring at her with glinting eyes. "You involved someone else in our war, and that's something I won't stand for."

"No. I didn't."

The quiet denial drained his anger away. His eyes narrowed, probing her delicate face. "You went out with Sinclair."

"I had lunch with him." Heather pushed her hands into the pockets of her robe and met his gaze levelly. A small voice in her mind warned that she was a fool to explain the matter to him, but she ignored it. She knew herself to be unequal to the task of coping with a repeat of his earlier rage.

"You had lunch with him in his penthouse."

"I had to talk to him privately." She saw Adam stiffen

88

slightly and went on in a calm voice. "He and my room-mate split up several weeks ago, and I was trying to get them back together."

"And that remark of his when you got out of the car?"

Heather looked blank for a moment and then remembered what Alex had called out to her as she had started toward the office. She shrugged. "Alex was grateful. He said that he and Lisa would name their first child Heather."

"You little witch," Adam muttered softly. "You deliberately let me believe that Sinclair was your lover."

She shook her head, one brow lifting wryly. "The idea was yours. I just didn't deny it."

The black eyes glittered with humor or irritation—she wasn't sure which. Huskily he said, "That's hitting below the belt, sweet Heather. Not fair."

Heather felt an odd little leap of her pulse as she watched him smile crookedly. Trying to ignore the sensation, she grimaced slightly. "Why is it that all my weapons are unfair and all yours aren't?" she demanded half angrily.

He laughed softly. "Would you like to lay a few ground rules," he asked without answering her question, "so that we both know where we stand?"

Heather made one last attempt to reason with him. "Don't you think this has gone far enough? The next couple of weeks are going to be hectic enough at the office without—"

"Which brings me to rule number one," he interrupted calmly. "Until things settle down at the office, we declare a truce. Agreed?"

"Agreed," Heather said at once, thanking God for small favors. At least she'd have a breathing spell!

Dryly Adam murmured, "I thought you'd like that one. Rule number two: No outside aid. This is just between the two of us. Agreed?"

A little more slowly this time, Heather said, "Agreed."

Adam folded his arms across his broad chest and stared at her consideringly. "Rule number three: We keep up appearances at the office. We act polite, if not friendly. Agreed?"

"Agreed." Before he could go on, Heather said flatly, "Rule number four: No more sneak attacks. Agreed?"

A faintly mocking smile creased his lean face. Humor gleamed in the black eyes. "It served its purpose," he murmured, as if to himself. "Agreed," he said finally.

There was a long silence as the two stared guardedly at each other. Tension stretched between them, the tension of two people who have admitted their physical attraction for each other but have no intention of giving in to it. It was an almost tangible thing, like a rope of silver threads tying them together in an ever-tightening bond.

It made Heather nervous. She moved suddenly, restlessly, dropping her eyes from his intent gaze. "Now that we've got that settled," she murmured, "would you mind leaving?"

"I don't suppose it would do any good to ask if you'll have dinner with me tonight," he said ruefully.

She looked up, an indignant refusal on her lips, but something in his face made her pause, uncertain for the first time. Damn the man! How did he manage to look so ridiculously hopeful? When she finally responded, it was in a surprisingly mild voice. "Not tonight. I'm very tired."

He nodded slightly, unsurprised, accepting her refusal with unwonted meekness. "Will you at least walk me to the door?" he asked with a whimsical smile.

Suspicious, Heather nodded and silently accompanied him to the door. As she stood aside for him to pass, her eyes widened slightly when he paused in the doorway. One large hand reached to gently tilt up her face.

"May I kiss you?"

For the second time that day Heather had the bewildered feeling that her mouth was hanging open. "What?"

His voice was soft, incredibly tender. "No sneak attack, Heather. Just a simple request. I would like very much to kiss you good night. May I?"

Heather couldn't answer him. She gazed upward, drowning in the velvety black pools of his eyes. Involuntarily she swayed toward him, her eyes closing as his dark head bent toward hers. After a slight hesitation, a soft intake of breath, she felt his lips gently brush her forehead.

"Sweet dreams, Heather."

Her eyes snapped open in astonishment as the doorknob was gently pulled from her grasp. She stared at the closed door for a long moment, a flush staining her cheeks as she realized what she had done. Oh, for God's sake, was she bewitched by this man? She felt like a fool. A prize idiot. He was probably laughing at her.

And why not? She had just agreed to a set of ground rules with a man whose purpose was to seduce her! She needed to have her head examined.

She brushed aside the upsetting thought, deciding to forget the whole baffling business, at least for tonight. She piled records on the stereo, unconsciously choosing dreamy romantic ballads, then went to the kitchen to prepare herself a light meal of a salad and an omelette.

After cleaning up in the kitchen, she went back into the living room and curled up on the couch. She rested there silently, limp, weary, listening to the emotional love songs coming from the stereo. It was some moments later when her nose twitched slightly and she looked around the room with a puzzled frown. Roses? There weren't any roses in the room. Why did she smell roses?

Her eyes settled at last on her purse, lying on the couch beside her, and she reached over slowly to open it. Inside were two delicate flowers. She drew the flowers out carefully, staring at them with startled eyes. One was a maiden's blush rose, its petals still tightly curled into a heart-shaped bud. The other was a purple columbine.

Two flowers chosen at random? The rose because it was a traditional symbol of romance, the columbine because it matched her eyes?

Somehow Heather felt that it was more than that. Flowers had been a childhood hobby of hers, and she knew that each flower had a meaning. But did Adam know? It would explain the columbine, which not only matched her eyes, but meant resolved to win. That was a message she could easily understand.

But the rose? Was it a message as well? And, if so, what did he mean by "If you love me, you will find me out?"

Find him out? That didn't make sense. Staring down at the flowers in her hand, Heather sighed softly and acknowledged to herself that nothing about her odd relationship with Adam made any sense.

She didn't want to think about the first part of the rose's meaning. If you love me . . . But she didn't love him; she didn't even *know* him! Her heart was untouched. Untouched. She repeated the thought as if it were a talisman to ward off love and all its complications. She didn't want to fall in love, and most especially not with Adam Blake. He wanted no ties, no commitments. Only her body.

Her gaze focused on the flowers. Why the chaste kiss on her forehead tonight? And why the romantic gesture of flowers—whatever their meanings? His gentleness . . .

It hit her then with the suddenness of a blow. Of course! He was simply changing tactics. Damn him! He was launching an attack of pure guile, expressly designed to undermine her determination. He intended to lull her into a false sense of security. He would be polite and charming, she decided grimly, hoping that his change of attitude would knock her off guard. Perhaps he even intended to make her fall in love with him.

No way! She had caught on to his little tricks now, and Adam Blake could go hang if he expected her to fall for them. She would be doubly on guard from now on, suspecting every move he made. He would not win. *He would not.*

She was asleep when Lisa came home that night, the flowers pressed between the pages of a book on her nightstand—an action which she didn't care to question herself about.

The next morning Heather walked to the office, enjoying the early spring weather. Reaching the building, she went in and waved absently to the guard as she headed for the elevator. Once on her floor, she moved down the long hall, noticing that no one seemed as tense as they had the day before. So, she mused sardonically, he's already started charming the help. Now everyone will probably start bending over backward to please him.

The thought irritated Heather. She went into her office, noting that the inner door was open and Adam's office empty. Sitting down at her desk, she notified the switchboard that she had arrived, and then uncovered her typewriter and finished the letters she had not had time for yesterday. She had just pulled the last of these from the machine when Adam entered the office.

"Good morning, Heather." He greeted her calmly, then, before she could respond in kind, went on briskly. "Get your notebook and come into my office, will you please? There are a couple of letters I want to send out this afternoon." Again, without waiting for a response, he continued on to his office.

Automatically Heather gathered up her notebook and pencil, then went into his office and sat down in front of the desk. She barely had time to open the notebook before he started dictating, and her fingers flew in order to keep up with him. But she did not have to ask him to wait while she caught up—a source of silent pride to her. He was as good as his word, dictating two letters and then politely, if a bit abruptly, requesting that she have them ready for him to sign by lunchtime.

As the day wore on, Heather grew more and more bewildered. She told herself that his businesslike attitude was a welcome relief, but something inside her was irritated by his terse formality. Not a single personal word had been exchanged between them.

The pattern of that day was repeated the next day and the next. Adam continued to be terse and businesslike, evincing no interest whatsoever in the attractions of his secretary. In fact, Heather began to doubt that he saw her as a woman at all. He seemed more inclined to view her in the light of a particularly useful piece of office furniture. Not by a single word or gesture did he indicate that he even remembered the violent emotions that had raged between them on Monday.

The situation should have pleased Heather. It didn't. She had expected him to charm her, and he charmed her about as much as he charmed his desk. It was maddening. A part of her waited warily for his pounce. Another part of her believed, with a surprising sense of disappointment, that he had lost interest in the battle. Perversely she found that she was intrigued by this new facet of the man. It was a fascination that irritated as much as it compelled, but Heather was powerless to fight it.

She found herself observing him covertly during those next two days. Watching him, listening to the deep voice issuing curt orders, she was forced to revise her first impression of him as a jet-setting playboy.

In two days he had smoothly assumed control of the company, gaining the respect and admiration of everyone he dealt with. That charming smile of his—always directed at someone other than herself—made commands sound like requests, and even those employees filled with anxiety before his arrival were soon falling all over themselves to please him.

And Heather could have had two heads and been tinted a pale green for all the notice he took of her.

The tensions of the day followed her home, causing her to snap at Lisa for no good reason and brood a great deal. Leon had come over once, but Heather had been tired and irritated, and hadn't noticed his worried eyes following her as she moved restlessly around the apartment. Nor had she noticed Lisa drawing her father aside to whisper into his ear, or his startled response.

She had no way of knowing, as busy as she had been, that there was already a great deal of gossip concerning her relationship with the new owner of Norden. The tension between them on that first day had not escaped notice, or the fact that she had been driven home—or somewhere—by Adam.

Leon's offhand questions about her new boss had, therefore, drawn equally offhand replies. And not even to Lisa would she speak in anything but the most general terms about her employer. She resisted the gentle probing of her best friend with a stubbornness that had nothing to do with a lack of trust in Lisa, but rather with a lack of certainty in herself. She didn't know why she was brooding, or why her temper seemed frayed these days.

And she didn't know why her sleep was restless, her dreams disturbed. Or why she felt this peculiar aching tension within her, increasing with each passing day. She didn't know.

Heather awoke on Friday with an oddly buoyant feeling that puzzled her until she reached the office. It was then that she remembered today was the day of Norden's retirement party, an event organized and paid for by the employees. A celebration—just what she needed! And if a Norden celebration couldn't cheer her up, then nothing could. The company was well known in San Francisco for its boisterous and somewhat frenetic parties in celebration of holidays or a lucrative new account.

Norden had always been very lenient about the parties, realizing that his hard-working employees needed to let off steam occasionally. Advertising was a hectic and competitive business, and tension built quickly; the parties were a needed safety valve. Apparently Adam was just as lenient —at least on this occasion. His memo decreed that the party would start at five P.M. and continue until the last hearty soul crawled out the door, a statement that caused a great deal of laughter and not a few embarrassed faces.

The day started out normally enough, for Heather at any rate. There were the usual letters to get out, the usual calls. Adam continued to be businesslike and formally polite. He didn't even notice that his secretary wore a blue silk dress (because of the party, she told herself) that made her look, according to Lisa, like Helen of Troy must have looked when she launched all those ships.

Heather told herself that his lack of interest didn't bother her in the slightest. That was probably why she banged the keys of her typewriter with unnecessary force. And slammed a drawer. Twice.

By the time four-thirty came, Heather's buoyant feeling had completely disappeared, and she gritted her teeth with a sensation of acute frustration when Adam told her absently that she could go now. It took every ounce of control she could muster to keep herself from bashing him over the head with the glass paperweight on his desk. Sanity prevailed, however reluctantly.

She went down to the cafeteria to find the party already in full swing. Music blared from a stereo; laughter rang out. Heather wondered wryly if Norden would appreciate the cheerfulness with which his leaving was being celebrated, then decided that he knew his former employees too well to be offended.

She threaded her way through the crowd until she

96

found Lisa, who was standing by the buffet cheerfully explaining to another photographer that she never photographed Norden parties for the company scrapbook because if she did no one would speak to her afterward. The other photographer turned away as Heather reached her friend.

Lisa shot a perceptive glance at Heather's tense face and inquired sympathetically, "Bad morning?"

Heather reached for the punch ladle and a cup. "Don't ask," she responded ruefully. "I might lose my head and answer you." She took a sip of the punch and nearly choked; it had been liberally spiked. She turned her gaze to Lisa's amused face. "I think it's going to be some party," she murmured.

As the evening wore on, Heather drank club soda, danced with several men, and managed, in spite of everything, to have a good time.

The party was a few hours advanced when the guest of honor arrived, accompanied by the new owner, and Heather tensed from head to foot. She remained tense while gifts were presented, toasts proposed, and hearty good wishes exchanged. She became even more tense when dancing resumed—for those who still could.

She needn't have bothered.

Adam moved from group to group, flirting lightly and cheerfully. He danced with some of the secretaries. He danced with some of the female executives and the male executives' wives. He even danced with Lisa. He did not dance with Heather. In fact, he didn't even seem to realize she was there.

He strolled out the door around ten, as sober as he had entered, without a backward glance.

CHAPTER SIX

On Saturday Heather went back to the gallery where she had first encountered Adam. The portrait of herself was gone, and the owner of the gallery, Andrews, refused to tell her anything about it. He was obviously startled at meeting the girl in the painting, equally curious about the whole thing, but he told her that he had been allowed to exhibit the painting only on condition that he reveal nothing of the artist.

Frustrated, Heather went home. She was bothered by that painting, even though she told herself fiercely that she simply could not have forgotten if she had been in love. It was plain to her that the artist, Hyde, had painted an idealized portrait of a woman in love, and she had been the model. That was all. But she had wanted to meet Hyde, because at least he could have told her where she was sometime during that six months.

Leon came over that night, telling his daughter and her roommate that he had decided to remain in San Francisco for a few weeks. He hadn't had a vacation in years; now was as good a time as any, he told them. He also wanted to spend time with his daughter, since she would be getting married in the fall.

It was the first Heather had heard of a wedding date, and she turned to Lisa in surprise. "Fall? But that's months away!"

Lisa, sitting on the couch beside her father, grimaced slightly. "I know. But Alex is all tied up with this strike right now, and once it's settled—if it ever is!—it'll take weeks to get his other business affairs in order. He's decreed that we're going to have a two-month honeymoon in Europe, so everything has to be settled here first." Without missing a beat she said, "And I wish you'd stop pacing, Heather."

Startled, Heather stopped the restless, unconscious movement. She sank down in a chair and avoided her friend's bright, inquisitive stare. "A two-month honeymoon in Europe," she murmured. "No wonder you're waiting."

Lisa disregarded this. "Heather, what's going on between you and Adam Blake?"

It was the first time Lisa had come right out and asked the question, and Heather was caught off guard. She glanced at Leon's calm, inquiring face, and then looked hurriedly away. "Nothing's going on, Lisa. It's just been a hectic week, that's all."

"The office has been hectic before," Lisa retorted flatly, "and you've taken it all in stride. But this last week you've been as jumpy as a cat. And, all that aside, Adam gave me a very peculiar message when he danced with me yesterday. A message for you."

"Message?" Heather's violet eyes widened, her body tensed visibly. "What kind of message?"

"I hope it means more to you than it did to me. For a moment there, I thought he'd had a bit too much of the punch," Lisa said ruefully. "He said: 'Tell your roommate that my new strategy appears to be paying off. She's outflanked and outgunned, and I should be raising the flag shortly.' "

"Why, that arrogant—" Heather began heatedly, then halted abruptly as both her friends stared at her in surprise.

"Obviously the message was understood." Lisa grinned. "Still want to tell me that there's nothing between you two?"

A little embarrassed by her outburst, Heather smiled wryly. "I'm not going to tell you anything." Her smile widened at Lisa's disappointed expression. "Not now, anyway. Later, when I've figured it out myself." Before her friend could respond, Heather resolutely changed the subject and began to talk about wedding plans.

It wasn't until later, as she lay wide awake in her bed, that Heather thought over Adam's message. So—he hadn't called off the war after all. He had simply come up with an unexpected and completely maddening strategy. And it had been effective.

Damn the man! She had expected charm and received indifference, a tactic calculated to drive any woman out of her mind. Beneath the businesslike attitude he had assumed all week, he had probably been watching every move she made. And his message had proven that he was completely aware of just how effective his strategy was.

Heather turned over in bed and buried her face in the pillow, trying to ignore her thoughts. Most especially she tried to ignore the realization that she had been relieved that Adam had not, after all, lost interest in the war.

She entered her office on Monday morning not knowing quite what to expect from Adam. But when he came in, greeted her casually, then went into his own office, she realized somewhat wryly that this day was to be a repeat of last week. She got down to work and grimly resolved that his new strategy would not undermine her own determination.

Only one thing occurred during the day to shake her resolve, and that happened just after lunch. Heather had gone down to the cafeteria to eat, and when she returned to her office, she found that Adam had not yet returned. It was past two o'clock when he finally came in and paused by her desk to collect his messages.

Suddenly he reached out to gently touch the small, crescent-shaped scar on her right cheek. "How did this happen?"

Taken completely by surprise, Heather started uncontrollably. She stared up at his expressionless face, painfully aware of his fingers against her face. "I had a car accident a few years ago."

He calmly tipped her face to one side, studying the tiny scar and then her entire face in an oddly detached manner. Finally, his black eyes unreadable, he murmured, "A human flaw. Yes, such unearthly beauty needs that tiny flaw to make it seem real." Then he picked up the messages and went into his own office.

Stunned, Heather sat perfectly still, feeling the same sensation of almost physical shock that she had experienced when Lisa had used that phrase in jest. Unearthly beauty? Why did those words disturb her so greatly? And why had Adam suddenly stepped out of his business-like role to say them?

It proved to be a temporary aberration. When Heather carried a few letters into his office minutes later for him to sign, he had reverted to his formal, distantly polite manner.

He called her into his office just before five, and she went in to find him talking to a client on the phone. Waiting silently in front of his desk, she listened to him coolly mapping out a campaign for the client that would probably make the man a fortune. Heather was impressed, although her expressionless face betrayed nothing.

Hanging up the phone, he looked up at her. Without

preamble he said, "I'm having a dinner party tomorrow night at my apartment for some of our major clients. There will be about twenty people. My houseman will see to the food. I want you to be my hostess."

"I can't do that!" Heather exclaimed involuntarily.

He frowned impatiently. "Of course you can. You've done the same for Norden; he told me so himself."

"Only when his wife was out of town," she retorted.

Adam sat back and regarded her with baffled eyes. "So what's the problem?" he inquired. "As it happens, I don't have a wife handy, and I need a hostess. You're elected."

Heather was beaten and she knew it. The last thing in the world she wanted to do was to play hostess for him, but it was not, under normal circumstances, an unreasonable request. She had, as he had remarked, often done the same for her former employer. And since Adam was so firmly encased in his businessman wrappings, she could hardly declare that she suspected his motives.

So gritting her teeth in frustration, she asked calmly, "What time?"

"Eight." Apparently deciding that everything was settled, he reached across his desk for a file, opened it, and began to study the contents. "I'll pick you up around seven thirty."

"I'll take a cab," she said quickly.

"Just as you like," he muttered absently. "Bayview Apartments, the penthouse."

Piqued by his indifference, Heather turned and left the office, closing the door with a little more force than was necessary. It wasn't until she was back at her desk that she realized irritably that she was letting him get to her. Oh, Lord! She was beginning to feel like a yo-yo! She told herself firmly that she much preferred the businesslike Adam to the seductive or mocking one, but the thought had little conviction. And she couldn't help wondering if he would pull yet another personality out of his hat and torment her with it. The man was an absolute chameleon.

She got through the next day somehow, rushing home at five to get ready for the party. A long hot bath helped to soothe her nervous tension, and by the time she had completed her makeup, she felt reasonably calm. She decided to wear her newest dinner dress—a pale blue chiffon creation with long, flowing sleeves, a V neck, and a low-cut back. The floor-length gown swirled gracefully around her slender ankles, showing off the delicate Italian sandals on her tiny feet.

Heather stood silently in her room, staring at her reflection in the mirror on the back of her bedroom door. The dress gave her an oddly ethereal appearance, fragile, fairy-like. Her hair was piled loosely on top of her head, a few strands allowed to frame her face in a softening effect. Her violet eyes were more brilliant than usual, and there was a soft, natural flush in her cheeks.

With a faint sigh she turned away from the mirror, wondering absently if Adam would notice how she looked tonight. She wanted him to. She didn't stop to question, to wonder why. She simply wanted Adam to think that she looked beautiful.

Heather left a note for her still-absent roommate on the refrigerator in case Lisa would wonder where she was, then picked up her evening purse and left the apartment. The cab that she had called earlier was waiting, and she was soon on her way to Adam's apartment.

Bayview Apartments, as the name indicated, overlooked San Francisco Bay. It was a large, modern building with wide, sunny terraces and an absurdly high rent—at least she had heard that.

She passed through the quiet lobby and rode the elevator up to the penthouse, her fingers grasping her purse nervously. She had never liked business parties, although she had gotten very good at them during the past two years. Her innate shyness made it difficult for her to meet and talk casually with new people, and only Norden's unshaking confidence in her had helped her to overcome her tendency to shrink into corners.

So she felt no particular anxiety about this party, except in regard to Adam. Who would he be tonight? she asked herself wryly. The formal businessman? The mocking devil? The seductive . . .

As the elevator doors opened on the penthouse floor, she cut her train of thought off abruptly. Squaring her shoulders in determination, she walked down the short hall to the apartment door and knocked on it. The door was opened almost immediately, and a middle-aged man with an impassive face gazed at her. Something very like surprise flickered for a moment in his eyes, and then he was bowing slightly. "Miss Richards?"

"Yes." She smiled tentatively at him.

He stepped back and swung the door wide. "Mr. Blake is still dressing, Miss Richards. I am Douglas, his houseman."

"How do you do?" Heather came inside the hall and watched as he closed the door behind her. "Mr. Blake said that you would handle the food. Is there anything I can do to help?"

He inclined his head slightly. "Thank you for the offer, Miss Richards, but everything is under control. Mr. Blake asked that I show you the apartment, and then perhaps you will wait for him in the living room?"

Heather nodded, and then followed him down the hall, pausing to glance at each room as he pointed it out. The kitchen and dining rooms were on the left, a study-library and spare room on the right of the long hall. All the doors were open except for the spare room, and she wondered absently what was in that room as she passed.

Douglas opened a set of double doors at the end of the hallway, disclosing a sunken living room which was as large as her entire apartment. The carpet was deep burgundy and the furniture, consisting mainly of a pit grouping in the center of the room and occasional chairs, was off-white and plush. The entire bay side of the room was glass, with doors opening onto the terrace. Oils adorned the other walls, some signed by artists she recognized, some unknown.

Another hallway led off to the right of the living room; Douglas gestured slightly toward it. "The bedrooms, Miss Richards. If you'll allow me, I shall place your purse in the first bedroom to the right of the hall. The other ladies' things will be placed there also."

Smiling faintly, Heather handed over her purse and watched as he took it into the bedroom. When he reappeared, he said, "If you will excuse me, Miss Richards, I will return to the kitchen. Mr. Blake shall be with you shortly."

She nodded and, as he left the room, wandered over to the terrace doors. Tiny lights dotted the shores of the bay and were reflected off the water like a scene from a Christmas story. Heather stared down at the peaceful picture, her eyes dreamy. It was sometime later that she realized she was not alone. She turned suddenly, her eyes widening as she saw Adam standing just a few feet away, staring at her. Oh, God, she should have known he'd be devastating in a dinner jacket! And then she noticed the look in his eyes.

It was an odd look, somewhere between pleasure and pain, disappearing even as she noticed it. It was not replaced, however, by the aloof, indifferent expression with which he had gazed at her for the past week. The heavy-lidded eyes swept her body slowly, a tiny flame kindling in their velvety black depths, and Heather felt an answering fire burst to life somewhere within her.

His eyes moved slowly back up to her face, the fire in them no longer small. "Heather," he murmured with incredible softness, "sweet Heather. You're so beautiful. It astonishes me all over again each time I see you."

Heather felt the breath catch in her throat and her heart begin to pound with an uneven rhythm. She forgot their shared antagonism, forgot everything but the man staring at her with desire in his eyes. "I—thank you," she murmured huskily. He stepped toward her, and she noticed for the first time that he held a small spray of white flowers in his hand.

"May I?" He made a slight gesture toward her hair.

Confused, she nodded, only then realizing what kind of flowers he was pinning above her left ear. Acacia—white acacia. Was this a message too? Concealed love. No, he couldn't . . .

The flowers securely pinned, his hands came to rest on her shoulders, one thumb caressing her collarbone rhythmically. For a long moment he gazed at the bemused face turned up to his, his own face softened, tender. With a thread of rueful humor in his voice, he said, "Such a battle I've fought with myself this last week! You've no idea how hard it was for me to keep my hands off you."

It was an unfortunate choice of words. The conflict between them painfully recalled, Heather tried to step back and found that his hands, gentle as they were, wouldn't release her. "Lisa gave me your message," she told him breathlessly. "Your *new strategy!* And what is this? A more direct tactic?"

His fingers tightened slightly; his face went a bit grim for a moment. Then he was smiling wryly. "I've dug my own grave, haven't I?" he asked sadly. "You'll never believe me now, never believe anything I say."

"Can you blame me?" She stopped trying to get away from him, staring up at him guardedly.

His black eyes searched her face intently, a curiously somber look in their depths. "And if I told you I loved you?"

106

Heather felt her heart jump, but her voice was steady when she said, "I wouldn't believe you."

"Not even if I told you that I pace the floor at night because I need you so badly, that when I do sleep I dream of you, that I'd go out of my mind if I knew for sure that I would never be able to see you again? Would you believe me then?"

She was shaken by the yearning note in his voice, her determination weakened by a glow in his eyes that looked very much like adoration. Then she reminded herself bitterly that this was simply another of his tactics, and that knowledge enabled her to lift her chin and gaze at him steadily. "No. I wouldn't believe you."

His right hand slid down her arm to grasp her left hand, lifting it slightly, his thumb gently rubbing the third finger. Staring down at her hand, he murmured, "What can I do to convince you?"

Heather felt her fingers begin to tremble within his, a sudden hot-cold sensation rushing through her body. It was just a dramatic gesture, she told herself numbly, he wasn't implying marriage. *He wasn't.* And she was abruptly, overwhelmingly aware that she wanted to marry him more than anything else in the world.

God, oh, God, how had it happened? What evil fate had decreed that she was to fall in love with a man who only wanted her?

She veiled her eyes as he raised his, an automatic reaction, an instinct to hide the knowledge that would give him such power. He must not—could not—know.

"Heather?" He studied her expressionless face for a long moment, puzzled by her stillness, her lowered gaze. "It may be too soon, but, Heather, I—"

The doorbell rang, cutting him off abruptly. He glanced over his shoulder to see Douglas emerge from the kitchen and move toward the door, then sighed softly and stepped away from Heather, allowing his hands to fall. Almost inaudibly, he muttered, "I wonder who that bell saved, you or me."

The cryptic comment meant nothing to Heather; she barely heard it. She was fighting to control herself, fighting to understand how such a thing could have happened to her. Her mind felt numb, her body icy cold with shock. Her hands tightened into fists at her sides as she watched Adam moving toward the hall to greet his guests. And then he was turning to her with that charming smile, telling the owner of a West Coast wine company, "I'm sure you've met my assistant, Heather Richards."

And Heather found herself moving forward with a polite, social smile on her face, the turbulent emotions hidden out of sheer necessity. "Mr. Brewster, it's so good to see you again. Mrs. Brewster . . ."

It went on that way. The guests had all arrived within ten minutes, and Heather circulated among them, smiling, discussing campaigns and slogans and the latest marketing trends. Douglas took care of bar duties. A maid—hired for the evening, Heather assumed—moved through the room with a canapé tray. It was a party like any other that Heather had attended during the past two years.

Except for the presence of Adam Blake. He, too, circulated among his guests, lean and shatteringly handsome in his dinner jacket. And if the clients present had not already been won over by his business acumen, they were certainly captivated by his charm tonight.

Heather did everything in her power to ignore the effect that his charm had on her. But she couldn't help the way her heart thudded in double time whenever she heard his voice, and she couldn't prevent her eyes from searching for him whenever she couldn't hear him. She was aware of speculative glances being cast from her to the new owner of Norden, but she kept her social smile fixed upon her lips and tried to ignore those as well.

By the time dinner was announced, Heather was a bundle of nerves. She was grateful for the opportunity to sit down, although she was disturbed by the fact that Adam was directly in her line of vision at the opposite end of the long table. Wine was served with dinner; she barely tasted hers, just as she had barely tasted the drink she had carried around all evening. It was a temptation, though, to drown her sorrows. No wonder some people drank too much.

Dinner went on and on, forever it seemed. She talked lightly and casually to the men on either side of her, hardly noticing when the gentleman on her left—a single, middle-aged man who owned a sailboat firm—began to flirt with her. She responded to his overtures absently, trying to keep her gaze from shifting to the other end of the table.

But in her attempt to hide her emotions, Heather had unknowingly recaptured her other-world expression, and that only added heat to Dailey's suddenly conceived passion. He wanted her. And he was a man accustomed to getting what he wanted.

When the guests filed back into the living room, therefore, he literally cornered Heather near the terrace doors. She was not frightened by his persistence; this sort of thing had happened to her before at business parties. But she was hamstrung in her attempts to get away from him because he was an important client and one, moreover, who took offense easily.

So she backed away from him cautiously, now totally conscious of what was going on, determined to do nothing to cause a scene. Wryly aware that Dailey was drinking heavily and not responsible for his actions, she ignored the increasingly crass propositions and shifted to avoid his wandering hands. Then she found herself trapped, backed up against the wall. "Mr. Dailey, I really don't think—"

Her verbal plea was interrupted suddenly as a hand came down on Dailey's shoulder and he was pulled back away from her with something just short of physical violence. "Leave her alone, Dailey," Adam ordered curtly.

Either Dailey considered that he had nothing to lose, or else he believed implicitly in the old adage that in advertising the client possessed all the power. Or it was the liquor talking. "Stay out of this, Blake! It's between the lady and myself."

"The lady's a guest in my home, Dailey, and so are you. Leave her alone," Adam responded tautly.

Unpleasantly Dailey said, "Can't you see when you're not wanted, Blake? I think the lady's just playing hard to get." He laughed crudely. "She'll come around soon enough, they always do!"

Heather saw Adam's hands clench into fists, and her heart jumped into her throat. Everyone in the room was staring. Oh, God, and she had wanted to avoid a scene!

"Get out of here, Dailey." Adam's voice was dangerous in its very softness, cutting through the sudden silence in the room, as though he had shouted. "You aren't welcome in my home."

Dailey's broad face flushed with rage; his bloodshot eyes glittered. "Oh, I see," he said loudly, nastily. "She's already staked out as private property, isn't she, Blake?"

Adam moved suddenly, and by sheer instinct Heather stepped between the two men, facing Adam. Gazing up at him, one hand unconsciously resting against his broad chest, she whispered, "Please, Adam, it isn't important."

Two pairs of eyes, one dark and oddly bemused, the other soft and pleading, locked together. Heather was vaguely aware of Douglas firmly leading the client out of the room, vaguely aware that the guests had resumed their conversations. She couldn't tear her eyes away from Adam's.

His hand came up to cover the one resting against his chest. "That's the first time you've said my name," he said huskily.

110

Heather's tongue appeared to wet suddenly dry lips, unconsciously drawing his attention to her mouth. She felt the heat of his look as if it were a brand, her body catching fire with the explosive suddenness of dry timber. Helpless to deny the turmoil within her, she stared up at him, her eyes darkened with need.

"Oh, damn," he muttered hoarsely, "why aren't we alone?"

Recalled to her senses, Heather stepped back abruptly and pulled her hand away from his grasp. "We—we're neglecting the guests," she murmured unsteadily.

He continued to stare at her, unconscious—or uncaring —of the fact that though conversation had resumed in the room, the attention of his guests was still focused on the corner. "Shall I send them away?" he asked softly, seductively.

"Don't be ridiculous," she responded firmly, turning away from him with an effort that was painful, and beginning to circulate among the guests again. She was uncomfortably aware of curious eyes skating away from hers abruptly, but there was little she could do about it. Tiredly she wondered how soon gossip concerning her relationship with Adam would hit the local newspapers. Tomorrow, probably.

For the most part she was spared open probing from the clients, although one client's wife did say bluntly when Adam was out of hearing that Heather was smart to latch on to a rich man who was still young enough to be exciting. Heather met the remark with blank eyes and silence, cringing inwardly at the nosedive her reputation had taken. The client hushed his wife with a look and smiled apologetically at Heather before she moved on.

She stayed as far away from Adam as she could in the room, not even looking at him if she could avoid it. She was furious with herself for having betrayed her desire so clearly, especially in front of all these people. God knew that Adam had seen her desire from the very beginning; it was the one thing she had never been able to hide from him. She was ashamed of her lack of restraint around him, appalled by her almost overwhelming urge to fling herself into his arms and give him anything he wanted.

Bitterly, she asked herself what chance she had with a man whose ability to bewitch could easily rival Merlin's. None. No chance at all.

Anger. That was it! She had to get angry at him. It was her only defense. Why couldn't she get angry at him?

It was midnight before the last guest finally left, and Heather backed nervously away from the door as Adam closed it and leaned back against it. "I . . . if you'll call me a cab—" she began.

He shook his head slowly, staring at her. "Not just yet," he murmured huskily. "There's a debt I have to collect."

She backed another step. "Debt? I—I don't know what you're talking about."

Softly he said, "Those beautiful eyes made me a promise tonight, sweet Heather. I won't let you back out on that promise."

Douglas appeared suddenly behind Heather after clearing up in the living room. Without betraying, by so much as the flicker of an eye, that he sensed the tension in the hallway, he asked calmly, "Will there be anything else tonight, sir?"

Hastily Heather said, "Could you call me a cab, please, Douglas?"

With a meaningful smile at his houseman, Adam said quietly, "I'll see Miss Richards home, Douglas. That'll be all."

With a nod the houseman disappeared into the kitchen, letting the door swing silently behind him.

Her attempt at escape foiled, Heather turned and went into the living room, trying frantically to whip up an anger she didn't feel. As Adam came into the room behind her,

112

she tried to be angry with him. "You shouldn't have made a scene with Dailey. He was drunk; he wasn't responsible for his actions."

Adam perched on the back of the couch, his wry smile indicating that he knew a change of subject when he heard one. "If a man isn't civilized when he's drunk, he isn't civilized when he's sober. The company's well rid of him as a client."

Ignoring the second part of the speech, she said immediately, "That isn't true; alcohol just relaxes inhibitions."

"Then maybe I should try getting you drunk," he muttered dryly. "Your inhibitions are Victorian."

Heather's feigned anger suddenly became real. Her violet eyes became stormy. "Victorian? Well, you belong in the eighteenth century—rakes were common back then!"

"Oh, for God's sake," he growled, rising and coming toward her with a determined glint in his eyes.

Quickly Heather retreated behind a chair, keeping it between herself and him. "You stay away from me!" she demanded, silently cursing the betraying tremor in her voice.

He halted and stared at her, his face tightening. "Damn it, I won't chase you around the furniture like a scene from some bad movie!" he said with suppressed violence.

"Good!" she shot back defiantly. "Now, if you'll call me a cab, I'll be on my way."

He folded his arms across his chest, a baffled look entering the black eyes. "I don't understand you, Heather. Earlier tonight I could have sworn—"

"That I was weakening?" She forced a bitter laugh. "Well, you were wrong! I won't let you win!"

Shifting impatiently, he snapped, "Will you forget about that stupid war? I was a fool to start it in the first place. I'm talking about you and me, and the way we feel about each other. You wanted me tonight, just as I wanted you. You can't deny that."

113

Disregarding most of what he said, she retorted angrily, "I know exactly what you want! You made that perfectly clear the day we met!"

His face whitened slightly; a strangely subdued note entered his voice. "You don't trust me, do you?" he murmured.

"Even a novice on the battlefield knows one thing: never trust the enemy!" she responded flatly.

A sigh seemed to come from the very depths of his being; a muscle jerked erratically in his jaw. "All right," he said very quietly. "I can afford the luxury. I surrender, Heather. You've won." He spread his hands in a defenseless gesture, his eyes very bright. "Victory is yours."

She stared at him, her violet eyes stunned. "No," she whispered. "No, I don't believe you. It's a trick. Another trick." Locked in her uncertainty, she made no move when he came around the chair and grasped her shoulders gently.

"I'm a prisoner of war, sweet Heather," he breathed almost soundlessly. "What will you do with me?"

The violet eyes gazed at him numbly.

He made a rough sound under his breath suddenly, his dark head lowering until his mouth found hers. Desire, sharp and devastating, lashed through Heather's body, and she realized at that moment that she had been waiting for this all evening. No, all week. She had needed it, hungered for it. And now she knew why she had been tormented by an odd, restless ache for days.

His hands were unsteady as they moved up to release her hair from its pins, neither of them noticing when the delicate spray of white flowers fell to the floor.

The kiss was a demand, a plea, igniting a spark in her veins that spread and burned with all the savagery of a fire raging out of control. She didn't protest when he swept her up into his arms and carried her to the couch. She didn't want to protest. She was driven by the same needs that drove him, the same hunger. And nothing mattered except his touch, his lean body against her own.

He lowered her gently to the cushions and then joined her, his body half-covering hers. Feverishly, with an odd familiarity, Heather coped with his tie and then pushed the jacket off his shoulders, unaware when he shrugged it to the floor. She was caught up in a whirlpool of sensation, fiercely conscious of the tangy scent of his skin, the taut muscles of his back beneath her fingers, his heart pounding against her breast with the same untamed rhythm of her own.

His lips trailed slowly down her throat, concentrating the fire of his demand on the tiny pulse beating frantically beneath her soft, scented skin. "Don't hate me, Heather," he pleaded thickly. "I can't stand it when you look at me with anger in your eyes. Don't hate me, darling." One hand slid beneath her to release the zipper of her dress, then moved back around to slip the gown off her shoulders.

Mindlessly Heather let her arms slide from the flowing sleeves without even a token protest. She was suddenly conscious of a wanton desire to feel his eyes on her body, a shameless need to know that he found her beautiful. The primitive craving overpowered the embarrassment she would have felt when he unfastened the front clip of her bra and smoothed the lace aside.

He stared down at her fixedly, an expression in his black eyes that she'd never seen before. "Oh, *God,*" he muttered hoarsely. "I never thought I'd . . . Heather, you're so beautiful!" His hands came up to cup her breasts, thumbs teasing the rosy peaks to vibrant awareness. And then he was lowering his head, lips continuing the arousal that his hands had begun.

Heather felt her senses spinning off into a maelstrom. She moaned raggedly as waves of sweet tension splintered through her, conscious, as she had never been before, of

115

the empty ache within her. Her trembling fingers moved to unbutton his shirt, desperate to feel his bare skin against her own. Muttering her name hoarsely, his lips returned to hers in a kiss of scorching, ferocious passion.

As her fingers released the third button, she felt something warm and heavy fall to rest between her breasts, and realized immediately that it was the medallion he always wore. For some reason the realization brought sanity crashing through her mind.

What in God's name was she doing? He had tricked her! Damn him, he had tricked her! His unexpected "surrender" had thrown her off balance, and he had been swift to take advantage of her uncertainty. But even with the knowledge that he had deceived her, Heather found herself unable to fight him. Her body clamored for his possession, the fire within it burning more strongly than ever. She kept her eyes closed as his mouth slid down to ravage the soft flesh of her throat, tears squeezing out from between the long dark lashes.

With that odd perception that had surprised her more than once, he seemed to sense that something was wrong, lifting his head suddenly to stare down at her with clouded eyes. Silence stretched between them for a long moment, until Heather finally opened her eyes to gaze up at him, half afraid that she would see the rage she knew him capable of. But, strangely enough, he didn't seem angry.

What was the expression on his lean, handsome face, she wondered. Disappointment? Bafflement? Pain? Her bewildered mind could make no sense of it.

"Don't cry, Heather," he murmured finally, heavily, one finger touching her cheek fleetingly. "It was too soon, I know." He moved away from her to sit on the edge of the couch, then reached over and tenderly fastened her bra and drew her dress up over her shoulders.

His gentleness moved Heather oddly, on some level she couldn't quite reach. She lay in silence and stared up at him, her violet eyes dark and turbulent with emotions she didn't even try to name.

Adam just watched her for a moment, a brooding, secretive look in his eyes. Then he commanded softly, "Say my name, Heather."

Helpless to resist him, she whispered huskily, "Adam."

He gazed down at her, his face taut. Then, in silence, he lifted her left hand and pressed it to his lips. It was a strangely reverent gesture, brief, tender. He released her hand slowly and then bent over to pick up his jacket and tie from the floor. Quietly he said, "I'll go get your purse and then drive you home."

Heather sat up and swung her legs off the couch as he moved toward the hall to the bedrooms, feeling her hand burn where his lips had been pressed against it. Shaking off the sensation, she stood up and reached to zip her dress, vaguely glancing around the room.

Her eyes fell at last on the carpet by the chair that she had used to keep him at bay earlier. Crushed into the deep pile of the burgundy carpet was a small spray of once-white flowers, now browning, curling.

Chilled, Heather waited silently for Adam and, when he returned to the room, left the apartment with him wordlessly. Adam, too, remained silent during the drive. At her apartment building he walked her as far as the door, waiting while she unlocked it. As she pushed the door open he said quietly, "I don't want to see you in the office until tomorrow afternoon. Good night, Heather."

She glanced up at him fleetingly, murmured a soft good night, and went into the apartment.

CHAPTER SEVEN

Moving into the living room lit only with one lamp, Heather dropped her purse on the chair and then sank down on the couch. For a long time she gazed blankly into space, her face expressionless. Then, slowly, she leaned forward to open the cabinet beneath the coffee table, withdrawing a sketch pad and a box of charcoal pencils. Moving as if in a dream, she opened the pad, placed it on her knee, and chose a fine-pointed pencil.

With the pencil poised over the pad, she hesitated, a faint quiver disturbing her face. Gritting her teeth slightly, she began to sketch, using short, tentative strokes of the pencil. The bracelet bothered her; she switched it to the left wrist absently. Unencumbered, her hand moved rapidly, more surely. An ability which had lain dormant for three years came suddenly to life.

A face gradually took shape beneath her skilled fingers, lean, handsome, inherently seductive. Dark brows and sleepy eyes lent the face a curiously bold sensuality. Tenderly curved lips added softness. Heather gazed at the stark portrait for a long moment, then picked up a broad-tipped pencil and added still more softness to the face with subtle shading.

Behind her, Lisa said quietly, "That's very good."

Without turning Heather responded calmly, "Not really. It doesn't really capture all the facets of his personality. I wouldn't make a very good portraitist."

Lisa came around the couch and sat down beside her friend, wearing the short terry robe that made her look like any man's dream of leggy American womanhood. "You're in love with him."

Heather smiled faintly, sadly, staring down at her creation of Adam. "Funny, isn't it?"

"Is it?"

Absently using a thumb to blend the shading, Heather murmured, "Oh, yes. It's hysterical. The farce of the year."

Lisa frowned, studying the feverish brightness of her roommate's eyes, the pallor of her face. "Everyone at the office thinks you two are having an affair." It was a question.

Heather smiled mirthlessly, her gaze still fixed on the sketch. "The clients at the party tonight think so too. By tomorrow, it'll probably be announced in the gossip columns."

"Is it true?" Lisa asked bluntly.

Wryly Heather replied, "Not yet. But it's only a matter of time. I realized that tonight." She turned a faint smile to her friend. "I can fight him, but I can't fight myself."

After a moment, Lisa said, "This may sound a little odd, but why fight at all? I mean, obviously Adam cares for you; you're the first woman he's shown an interest in since—well, since whatever happened years ago. And he *has* been good for you, Heather."

"I know." She sighed softly. "But I can't give in to him, Lisa. It's hard to explain."

"But, if you love him . . ."

119

"That's why." Heather dropped her eyes to the sketch. "It's because I love him that I don't want an affair. I'm not a prude, Lisa, but I won't be just a body in a man's bed. Not even if I love him. It has to mean more than that, for him as well as for me. Otherwise it would be empty, meaningless."

Lisa sighed softly. "Well, no one can make this kind of decision for you, that's for sure. But don't be too hasty in condemning Adam, Heather. He makes me think of an iceberg. You know, most of him hidden beneath the surface. The ten percent you can see feels desire; God only knows what the other ninety percent feels."

Heather turned to her in surprise. "Funny, I've thought that about him. And sometimes I feel that I can almost see beneath the surface, almost reach him."

"But?"

"But then it's gone." Heather shrugged wearily. "Like tripping a light switch. Everything goes black again."

Lisa sent her a swift, searching look, but Heather didn't notice it. She closed the sketch pad and put it on the coffee table, then rose to her feet. "I'm a little tired. I think I'll go to bed. Adam told me not to come in until afternoon, so I'll probably sleep late. Good night, Lisa."

"Good night." Lisa watched as her roommate left the room, then leaned over and picked up the pad. She opened it and stared for a long time at the face of Adam Blake. Almost inaudibly she murmured, "You woke her up, brought her back to life. And your face was the first thing she sketched in three years. I wonder. I wonder . . ."

Contrary to her wishes, Heather woke early the next morning, at her usual time. A glance at the clock on her nightstand made her groan and bury her face in the pillow, determined to go back to sleep. But nearly ten minutes of concentrated effort proved useless. And Heather was almost glad. Sleep was becoming an ordeal for her. Her dreams had been curiously vivid, disturbing.

120

Heather slid from her bed, pushing her dream from her mind. She put her robe on and went into the kitchen, finding Lisa dressed and sitting at the table with coffee and a newspaper.

"I thought you were going to sleep late."

"I'm slept out." Heather poured herself a cup of coffee and came over to the table and sat down. "If you've finished with the comics, let me have them. I could use a good laugh."

"Well, don't read the gossip column then," Lisa advised wryly.

Heather burned her tongue with an unwary swallow of the hot coffee and raised watery eyes to her friend. "Oh, God, didn't anyone ever teach you to give notice of loaded statements?" she asked breathlessly and, without waiting for a response, went on immediately, "Gossip column? You mean already?"

Lisa pushed the paper across the table to her. "One of Norden's esteemed clients must have gone straight from the party to the newspaper office."

Amazed, Heather read the damning sentences aloud.

> What handsome young advertising magnate, newly arrived from the East Coast, has managed to light a fire beneath San Francisco's own Ice Princess? And we thought she could do no wrong!

She looked up at Lisa wryly. "From Ice Princess to fallen woman in two lousy sentences! You'd think they could find something better to write about."

Lisa shrugged. "You've become pretty visible to the society snoops, you know. What with Norden's parties during the last two years, and you representing him at some of the big society bashes, you've been noticed. And since your reputation has always been one of . . ."

"Chastity?" Heather asked when Lisa's voice trailed off.

121

Lisa grinned. "Chastity. If you want my opinion, I'm surprised they wrote as little as they did. I would have expected them to say cute things about how the mighty are fallen or something."

Heather sighed. "It must be a sign of the times. A woman who doesn't sleep around seems to be considered a nearly extinct specimen. Why do I feel like a dinosaur?"

"Not a dinosaur, an anachronism." Lisa lifted one brow in amusement. "Out of step with the times, marching to a different drummer, and all that."

"*You* don't sleep around, but I don't see them calling you the Ice Princess!"

"Ah!" Her friend raised a triumphant finger. "But I'm not in the spotlight, which is where Norden put you two years ago when he made you his assistant. Besides, if I have a reputation for anything, it's carelessness, not coldness."

Heather looked faintly troubled. "Coldness? Have I really been that bad, Lisa?"

"Not anymore," Lisa responded cheerfully. "This column just shot that theory full of holes." After a moment she went on more seriously. "Don't worry about seeming cold, Heather. You've changed so much during the past two weeks that you're a completely different person. Not cold at all."

The reassurance helped until Heather looked back down at the newspaper; then depression swamped her. "How in the world am I supposed to face everyone at the office? This stupid column will seem like a confirmation of all the rumors."

"That depends. Do you want to look like a scarlet woman or an innocent victim?"

Heather frowned in faint irritation. "You seem to find the whole thing terribly amusing."

Lisa laughed softly. "Oh, I do. I've been waiting for two years for someone to wake you up. I was hoping it would be Daddy, but I have to admit that I like Adam. He seems like a nice guy, and he's certainly handsome."

In a wry voice Heather remarked, "A lion is a beautiful animal and seems gentle enough—until you put your hand through the bars of his cage."

"Wear leather gloves," Lisa grinned.

"Thanks a lot, friend, but your advice is a little late. No gloves ever made can help me now." Absurdly cheered by Lisa's lighthearted view of the situation, Heather felt a smile of real amusement tug at her mouth. "And my whip and chair seem to have disappeared as well. From this point on it's a bare-handed struggle."

Pleased to have lifted her friend's depression, Lisa remarked cheerfully, "Well, you can always buy a pistol and shoot him!"

"Don't tempt me."

Laughing, Lisa rose and carried her coffee cup over to the sink. "I have to go to work. Are you going to wait until afternoon to go in, or what?"

Heather got to her feet with a rueful smile. "I might as well get ready and go in this morning, otherwise I'll lose my nerve."

"Meet me for lunch?" Lisa turned with a mocking smile. "Unless of course you get a better offer!"

"I won't." Heather shrugged. "In the office he doesn't get any closer than three feet and projects a wall of formality that would daunt a seasoned diplomat."

"Disappointed?" Lisa asked shrewdly.

"Relieved." Heather's firm response was belied by the wistful expression in her eyes.

"Sure you are," Lisa scoffed lightly and then went on before her friend could respond. "Well, if you do by chance get a better offer, give me a call, okay?"

"Sure." Heather watched as her friend left, then went into her bedroom to get ready to go to work.

All the time she was dressing, Heather tried to build up

her defenses against Adam. She told herself that his "surrender" had been nothing more than a ruse, a deception to catch her off guard. She told herself that his "what ifs" before the party had been just another of his unscrupulous tactics, that he had not implied love or marriage. She told herself that he had halted his lovemaking because he knew how to bide his time, and not because her tears had moved him. She told herself that he felt only desire for her.

But she couldn't forget the flowers he had pinned in her hair. And she couldn't forget his whispered plea that she not hate him. Or the expression in his eyes as he had pressed her hand briefly to his lips. Or his gentleness.

She reached the office only an hour later than her usual time, not surprised to find that her coworkers had quite definitely read the morning paper. Pinning a calm smile on her face, she made no effort either to confirm or deny the speculation running riot through the entire building. Sly questions as to whether or not she had read the paper were answered with a cool affirmative, and she met the curious stares with unreadable eyes. She understood too well the nature of gossip, and had no intention of adding fuel to the fire with heated denials. It was enough that she knew the truth.

Once at her desk, Heather found that some helpful soul had left a copy of the paper there. Sighing softly, she stared down at the paper, opened and folded at the appropriate page, of course.

As she continued to gaze at the paper, the outer office door opened and Adam strode into the room. He stopped before her desk, frowning slightly. "I thought I told you not to come until afternoon. It's barely ten o'clock."

In a deliberately offhand voice, Heather said, "Oh, I thought that I'd come in early so everyone would have a little more to talk about during lunch."

Baffled, Adam asked, "Have I missed something?"

"Have you read the morning paper?" Heather didn't look at him.

"No."

"Then you've missed something." Heather pushed the newspaper across the desk toward him. "I'm sure you'll want to cut this out and paste it in your scrapbook."

Adam leaned a hip on her desk as he read the column, and she waited for his response. It was not quite what she had expected.

"Handsome. That's very flattering."

Irritated, she glared at him. "Is that all you have to say? That you're flattered?"

With a maddening expression of patience on his lean face, Adam asked, "What do you want me to say?"

It was an unanswerable question and, confused, Heather took refuge in anger. "My reputation was impeccable until you came along!"

"Really?" His black eyes brooded down on her. "Did you enjoy being called the Ice Princess?"

Heather rose slowly to her feet, feeling a sudden bitter rage envelop her. "Well, it was a lot better than being called your mistress," she told him tautly. "At least, before, I could hold my head up when I walked down the street!"

His head snapped back as though she had slapped him, the black eyes flaring. For a moment she was deeply and utterly afraid of what he might do. But then he straightened and tossed the newspaper across the desk. "Before you cast all the blame onto me, you'd better consider something, Heather," he said coldly. "Whoever tipped the newspaper didn't do so because of what happened between Dailey and me, but because of the way you looked at me. So if you don't want to be thought of as my mistress, don't look at me with bedroom eyes in public."

With an impulse beyond thought or reason, Heather's hand lashed out to strike him sharply across the face, the sound shattering the quiet of the office like the crack of a gun. Immediately her tingling hand came up to cover her mouth, her violet eyes wide with horror. "Oh, God, what are you doing to me?" she whispered.

Inexplicably he was not angry by the slap. While the imprint of her fingers slowly disappeared from his cheek, he stared at her in silence, a curious crooked smile on his lips. Then, quietly, he said, "Now we're even. But don't slap me again, Heather. Especially when what I'm saying is the truth."

"It wasn't!"

"Oh, no?" One slanted brow rose mockingly. "Believe me, Heather, I know desire in a woman's eyes when I see it."

"You saw what you wanted to see!" she accused bitterly.

"No." The black eyes took on that brooding expression which made her wary and nervous. "I didn't see what I wanted to see. I saw what was there. If I had seen what I wanted to see . . ." His voice trailed off into silence.

Stubbornly Heather refused to ask the question. She knew the answer. He had wanted to see love in her eyes, but not because he himself felt it. But he wanted her to feel it because that would be the signal that he had won, totally and completely. And it was a signal she never intended to give him.

He gazed at her shuttered face, the unreadable violet eyes, and sighed softly. "That's it," he muttered wryly, "keep the guard up. Never let yourself feel, because then you'd be human like the rest of us poor mortals."

She didn't rise to the bait this time. "Are there any letters to go out this morning, Mr. Blake?" she asked formally.

"You called me Adam last night." The remark sounded almost weary.

126

"I did a lot of foolish things last night." She looked at him levelly. "It won't happen again."

Very quietly he asked, "What do you want, Heather, a ring and a promise?"

Another tactic! she thought bitterly. "I can't be bought by rings," she replied flatly. "And your promises don't impress me."

"I see." Without another word he turned and went into his office, closing the door with awful quietness behind him.

Strangely Heather felt that a turning point in their relationship had been reached. Uncertainly she stared at the closed door, wondering why she felt suddenly empty inside. And alone.

Adam came out of his office a few minutes later, his face taut, eyes hooded. "If there are any calls, have them leave a message," he said flatly. "I'm going out for a while." Without waiting for a response, he left.

Heather got down to work, telling herself fiercely that she had been right not to believe the implication of his quiet question. He didn't want to marry her. A man didn't marry a woman only because he desired her. And he certainly didn't love her!

Adam came back shortly before lunchtime, offering no explanation for his absence. Heather asked for none. Determinedly she remained formal with him, disturbed when she realized that he had no intention of assuming his own businesslike formality. He watched her with brooding eyes, spoke to her tersely, almost rudely.

Heather should have been elated at this obvious evidence of his belief in her rejection, but she was worried. Adam was neither sullen nor resentful; he was the type of man who could shrug off a woman's rejection, accept it gracefully. But the stormy look in his eyes was not the look of a man either accepting rejection or denying it.

It was the look of a man at the end of his rope. He was

tense, restless, short-tempered. Annoying little problems that he would have dealt with calmly the day before roused him to anger today. He grew worse as the afternoon wore on, his temper becoming so brittle that Heather jumped every time he came into the room.

She hurriedly straightened her desk at five, determined to leave before he said anything to her, but just as she pulled her purse from the bottom drawer of her desk, he came out of his office. Without a word he caught her wrist in an iron grip and led her from the room, ignoring her gasp of protest.

Heather felt her cheeks begin to burn as he hauled her down the long hallway, painfully aware of startled, curious looks coming from the offices they passed. "What do you think you're doing?" she hissed in outrage, trying desperately to pull her wrist from his grasp.

"We have to talk," he replied shortly. "Alone."

Abandoning the useless attempt to get away from him, Heather hurried to keep up with his long strides, having no desire to look any more foolish than she had to. "Where are you taking me?"

"My apartment." He pulled her into the open elevator and pushed the button for the lobby. "We won't be interrupted there."

"I'm not going to your apartment!"

He looked down at her, the black eyes burning. "You'll go willingly or I'll carry you. The choice is yours."

Heather swallowed hard. "I'm not impressed by these caveman tactics, you know," she managed defiantly.

"I'm not trying to impress you."

The flat statement silenced Heather. His moody strength frightened her, but she was more frightened of herself. She didn't want to be alone with him in his apartment. She was too afraid of the way he made her feel when she allowed herself to respond to him. And she was very much afraid that if he took her in his arms one more time, she would be helpless to deny him.

She glanced up at him as they left the elevator and crossed the lobby, wondering tormentedly what had possessed her to fall in love with this man. And how could she fight him when her only defense was anger—an anger he could smother with a single kiss?

He led her to his car, putting her in the passenger side with a terse "Stay put" and then circling to the driver's side. He got in and started the powerful car with a roar, pulling out of the parking lot and into the stream of traffic with a complete disregard for the screaming tires and blaring horns of other drivers.

Heather closed her eyes tightly, her heart jumping into her throat as he continued to drive with reckless speed. Since her accident she had not driven a car, and high speeds terrified her. It did no good to tell herself that he was probably a very good driver. "Oh, please," she moaned finally, "please, slow down!"

He shot a glance at her paper-white face, the tightly closed eyes and immediately the speed of the car slowed to something approaching normal. Turning his own gaze back to the road, he murmured, "I'm sorry. I didn't mean to frighten you."

She felt her heart gradually return to normal and her muscles relaxed slowly. But by the time she could open her eyes, he was parking the car at his building. Silently she waited while he came around the car and opened her door. She made no protest when he led her into the building.

Once in his apartment, Heather walked into the middle of the living room and watched while he turned on a lamp. "Where's Douglas?"

"I gave him a few days off." Adam turned to stare at her broodingly. "So we're alone. Completely alone."

"Then say whatever it is you wanted to say and let me

go home," she said flatly, crossing her arms over her breasts and hugging her purse as if it were a shield.

He took a step toward her, his face tight. "I can't go on this way, Heather. Patience has never been my strong point, and what little I had went out the window long ago. How much longer are you going to dangle me on the end of a string?"

"I told you from the beginning that I would never become your mistress!" she snapped angrily.

"Are you going to let stupid pride come between us?"

"Us!" She laughed mirthlessly. "The only thing you're concerned about is *you!*"

"Is that what you really believe?" He took another step toward her, black eyes blazing.

"How can I believe anything else?" she shot back furiously. "Every time I look at you I'm reminded of exactly what you want of me!"

In a split second he had crossed the remaining space between them, ripping the purse from her grasp and catching her in an almost brutal embrace. Ruthlessly his mouth came down on hers, filled with rage and frustration.

Her hands caught between their bodies, Heather was powerless to push him away. But she fought. She squirmed frantically in his arms, keeping her mouth closed against him, determined not to give in. Her anger was her only weapon, fed by her desperate need to hide her love for him. His mouth ground savagely against hers, bruising her soft lips until her tongue detected the metallic taste of blood.

At that moment something snapped in Heather, and she went limp in Adam's arms, surrendering at last to a demand she could no longer ignore. Her body ached for his possession, her senses flaring with a sudden, agonizing pleasure. She wanted him. Her mouth parted beneath his, returning the savage kiss with wild abandon.

Her response did nothing to soothe his flaming desire;

130

it only increased it. He crushed her against the lean strength of his body, his mouth taking what she willingly gave. His lips burned a trail down her throat. "This is the one weapon you can't fight," he muttered hoarsely against her skin. "I can always make you want me, can't I, sweet Heather?"

Making no attempt to deny her desire, Heather pleaded huskily, "Not in anger. Please, not in anger."

He lifted his head, staring down at her with need written vividly on his face. "Not in anger," he promised softly, sweeping her easily into his arms and carrying her through the apartment to his bedroom.

With darkness falling outside, the room was dim and shadowy. He set her on her feet by the bed, his mouth lowering to gently tease her lips apart. Unsteady fingers slid around to unzip her dress. His gentleness melted the last of Heather's ties to reality, and she gave herself up mindlessly to the pleasure of his touch.

As the dress slipped from her shoulders, her hands rose to touch his face hesitantly, then moved down to open the buttons of his shirt. He groaned deep in his chest, his own hands smoothing away Heather's delicate underthings. "Yes," he murmured against her lips. "Touch me. I need you so much, sweet Heather." He lifted her naked body and placed her gently on the bed, straightening to rapidly strip off his clothing as he stared down at her with feverish eyes.

Heather lay in passion-drugged silence and watched him, feeling a peculiar pleasure in simply allowing herself to look at him. He reminded her, once again, of a lion in the prime of life, all tawny and muscled, his golden flesh gleaming in the dim light. As the clothing fell away from him, she caught her breath in wonder, oddly moved by his stark beauty.

And then he was beside her on the bed, his naked body hot and hard against the softness of hers. His hands moved

131

slowly down her body, mouth lowering to capture the hardened tip of one breast. His breath came harshly; a pulse pounded fiercely in his neck.

Heather gasped softly, her hands sliding over the muscles of his back. She felt a shudder wrack him, and knew that her body trembled in response. The ache inside her became a bittersweet pain, growing until it seemed to fill her entire body with its empty agony. She moved restlessly beneath him, biting lips already bruised and swollen from his heated kisses.

His caresses became more urgent; his body moved restively against hers. Feverishly his lips sought hers, then slid down to touch the frantic pulse beating beneath her ear. "Surrender to me, Heather," he groaned thickly. "Let me love you, darling."

An unreasoning fear gripped her as she heard the muffled words, a panic which she could not fight. No! She couldn't surrender to him! He would use her and then abandon her, and she couldn't bear to be left alone and empty again.

Again?

Desire fled as quickly as it had come. Heather stared at the ceiling with bewildered eyes. Confused thoughts raced through her mind, her body lay unresponsive beneath his.

"You're so beautiful," Adam whispered roughly, and then, sensing that something was wrong, he lifted his head. He stared down at her, his face draining of color as he saw her remote expression, her eyes fixed blankly on the ceiling. He swore softly, savagely, rolling away from her to sit on the edge of the bed. "Get dressed!" he commanded harshly. "I'll drive you home." Gathering his own things, he went into the connecting bathroom and slammed the door.

Like a robot Heather slid from the bed and dressed, dimly aware that her body was still aching, her limbs trembling. But her mind was a mass of turbulent questions, drowning every other sensation. *Again?* Why had her brain sent that final, desperate warning? What did it mean? Had she been hurt by a man? Was that the reason for her obsessive determination not to give in to Adam?

Oh, God. Had Lisa been right, after all? *Was* there a man in her past? Heather moved almost blindly into the living room and bent to pick up her purse from the floor. No. No, there couldn't be a man in her past. She would remember if there had been. She would remember. There had been no man. And the warning? Just the voice of sanity, she told herself fiercely, an instinct of self-preservation.

Adam came into the room just then, silently gesturing for her to precede him down the hallway. His face was white, eyes shuttered, every muscle in his body rigid. He didn't say a word.

Once in his car, Heather tried to think of some way of explaining her withdrawal to him, of convincing him that she had not deliberately set out to tease him. "Adam . . ." One hand reached tentatively toward his tense arm.

"Don't touch me, Heather," he warned tautly. "I won't be responsible for my actions if you do."

Her hand immediately dropped. Tears rose in her eyes. "I—I don't want you to think—" she began tremulously.

"Think what?" he interrupted coldly. "That you're doing your damndest to drive me out of my mind? Is that what you don't want me to think?"

"Adam, I couldn't help it, I—"

"You're not a child, Heather," he bit out savagely. "You know damn well what you did to me just now, and it wasn't pretty! Do you enjoy tormenting me, is that it?"

"No!"

"I think it is," he grated, his eyes fixed on the road ahead. "It was your intention from the first, wasn't it, sweet Heather?" His voice was hard, cold. "You weren't kidding when you said that you wanted total victory." He laughed harshly, the sound chilling Heather. "Well, raise the flag, because that's just what you've got. You're in my bloodstream now, under my skin, and I can't do a damn thing about it. I want you until nothing else matters, until I can't even think straight."

He pulled the car into the parking lot of her building and stopped. Half-turning in the seat to face her, he said flatly, "I'm on my knees, Heather. Happy?"

Her mind in turmoil, Heather reached for the door handle, desperate to be alone for a while and think. His hand grabbed her arm.

"Answer one question, Heather." He gave her a little jerk, so that she was forced to turn toward him. "Why?" When she continued to stare at him blankly, he repeated the question harshly. "Why? One moment you were completely with me, wanting to make love as much as I did. The next moment you were somewhere else. Does that calculating little mind of yours turn desire on and off like a switch, is that it?"

Without stopping to think, Heather burst out desperately, "I won't let you use me!"

Astonishment wiped away the anger on his face. "*Use you?*" he whispered incredulously. "Is that what you think —what you've thought all along?"

Suddenly uncertain, she whispered, "You told me that you wanted me in your bed. What else could I think?"

"You stupid little fool," he muttered, a burning anger kindling in his black eyes. "If you can't tell the difference between a man who wants to use you and one who wants to make love to you, then you're still a child." He dropped her wrist as if it burned him, his voice a whiplash. "Grow up, Heather! And when you decide to become a woman, give me a call. I won't hold my breath!"

Bewildered, Heather stumbled from the car, watching with stunned eyes as the car's taillights disappeared into the night. She turned toward the building slowly, his last words echoing in her mind. Oh, God, why did she suddenly feel like the villain?

CHAPTER EIGHT

A note on the refrigerator said that Lisa had gone out with Alex, something that relieved Heather. She had dreaded facing her friend's kind but inquisitive eyes. She changed into a loose robe and went into the kitchen, preparing herself an omelette which she knew would go uneaten. And, indeed, she barely tasted it before pushing the plate away with a faint grimace.

A movie on television failed to hold her attention, so did a recent best seller. Finally, in desperation, Heather took a sleeping pill around ten o'clock and went to bed, hoping that the morning would bring some order to her chaotic mind.

Her sleep was blessedly dreamless, and she woke long before her alarm went off. She was sitting at the kitchen table when Lisa came into the room nearly an hour later, drinking coffee.

Lisa lifted a surprised brow and glanced at the clock on the wall. "It's eight thirty and you aren't dressed. Aren't you going to work today?"

"Aren't you?" Heather countered, looking at her roommate's robe and pajamas.

Lisa shrugged and poured herself a cup of coffee. Carrying it to the table and sitting down, she replied, "I have to work Saturday, so I'm taking today off. How about you?"

"I'm taking the day off too." She didn't elaborate.

After a rather searching look, Lisa asked gently, "Did you know that you have a wicked-looking bruise on your arm?"

"I know."

"And you aren't going to tell me about it?"

"There's nothing to tell." Heather stared down at her coffee. "Nothing that you can't guess on your own anyway."

Lisa looked suddenly disturbed. "Adam? Heather, he didn't—"

"No, he didn't." She smiled faintly. "Please don't ask any questions, Lisa. The only reply I could give would be more questions." With a sigh she went on, "I've already called the office and talked to the Personnel Department. They'll get a replacement for me for today and tomorrow."

"What are you going to do?"

Heather shrugged. "Walk in the park maybe. I just need a little time to myself, Lisa." Almost inaudibly she murmured, "I have to decide whether to be a woman or a child."

After a moment of silence, Lisa said quietly, "I know sometimes we all have to be alone to sort things out, Heather, but if you need someone to talk to, I'm here. Remember that."

"Thanks." Heather got to her feet and smiled down at her friend. "I won't forget." She went into her bedroom and changed into slacks and a sweater and slipped her feet into espadrilles. She glanced into the mirror above her dresser, seeing a woman with huge, haunted eyes.

An hour later she found herself sitting on a bench in the

137

park, watching some children play. She had often come here when she was troubled, finding a peculiar peace in the laughter of happy children. But the magic didn't work today.

No matter how many questions she asked herself, it always came back to the same basic one: Could she take the chance that Adam's desire for her would grow into something stronger and more permanent? He had said that he wanted to make love to her, but was that just a euphemism for something far more basic, that is, lust? Or did he really care for her?

Could she bear it if she surrendered to him now, only to see him walk away when he grew tired of her? And could she bear it to walk away from *him*, never knowing the special joy of belonging to him, however briefly? It was no longer a question of resisting a strong physical attraction, she knew. It was a question of love, pure and simple. Her love.

And if she walked away from him now, she would be half alive, in limbo. What might have been would haunt her all the days of her life. And if she accepted the only thing he offered—a purely physical relationship—in the hope that love would grow, she would be taking the risk of watching her own love die a bitter death on some future day when he no longer wanted her.

Which would be worse? How could she choose the right path when both led to an uncertain and probably painful end? Existence in a limbo of loneliness, or existence in a world of moment-by-moment pleasure with the sword of Damocles hanging above her head?

The day wore on, and still Heather brooded, torn by conflicting impulses and desires. Childish laughter died away as mothers took their reluctant offspring home from the park, heading for baths and supper and bedtime stories. A light mist began, soon turning to a steady drizzle. Streetlights flickered on.

Heather was unaware of the passing hours. It was the steadily increasing rain that finally recalled her to her surroundings, the trickle of cold water down her neck jolting her from thought. She looked around in surprise at the dark, empty park, then glanced down to find her sweater plastered against her chilled skin. Her hair hung down her back in a sodden mass, fairly dripping with water.

She rose to her feet, wincing as stiff muscles protested in pain. Tiredly she wondered if pneumonia would set in and solve all her problems. Then her stomach audibly proclaimed its emptiness, and she added starvation to the list of possibilities. Idiot. She hadn't eaten since last night —and precious little then. If she had needed proof of her love, this was it; she was pining away for the man. Damn him. And damn her foolish heart.

She left the park, turning, when she reached the sidewalk, in the direction of her apartment. She had barely taken two steps when a silver-gray Mercedes pulled to the curb beside her. The passenger door opened. Adam was leaning across the seat to look up at her.

"Get in."

Without a word Heather obeyed the flat command, getting into the car and closing the door. Gripping her purse tightly on her lap, she stared straight ahead, wondering if he had come looking for her or if this was a chance meeting.

As if reading her mind, he answered the silent question brusquely. "I went by your apartment to talk to you after work. Lisa said that you'd gone out this morning and she hadn't seen you since. She told me that you came to the park sometimes." He shot a brooding look at her. "Are you so stubborn that you haven't the sense to come in out of the rain? You'll be lucky if you get out with nothing worse than a bad cold."

Heather ignored his comments, suddenly realizing that

the car was not heading for her apartment. "Where are we going?"

"My apartment. It's closer and you have to get out of those wet things as soon as possible." He didn't look at her, but he must have caught the swift, startled glance she threw at him. His mouth twisted. "Oh, don't worry, sweet Heather. I want a woman in my bed who knows her own mind and has no need for childish games."

Fighting a sudden urge to burst into tears, Heather stared through the windshield blindly. The bitter coldness in his voice chilled her, and she wondered if she did, after all, have a choice to make. Perhaps she had already driven him away from her.

Silence stretched between them during the remainder of the drive and the elevator ride up to his apartment. He unlocked the door and gestured for her to enter, his jaw-line taut and unyielding. Inside, he led her to the bedroom —his bedroom—and gestured toward the bathroom as he turned on a lamp beside the bed.

"There's a robe on the back of the door. Take a hot shower and put it on. Your things will probably dry in there as quick as anywhere else." He frowned as she stood, shivering, in the middle of the room. "Have you eaten anything today?"

She shook her head mutely, staring at him with disturbed eyes. He sighed. "I'll go and fix something. You get in the shower." He went out of the bedroom, closing the door firmly behind him.

Heather dropped her purse on a chair near the end of the bed and then moved into the bathroom. She turned on the light and closed the door, absently noticing the cream-colored robe hanging on the back of the door. Adam's, of course, and it would certainly swallow her whole. Looking into the mirror above the vanity, she grimaced slightly. No wonder he had been able to gaze at her with indifference— she looked like a drowned rat!

Quickly she turned on the shower and then stripped, hanging her things neatly on the towel racks. The hot water felt wonderful, and she stood perfectly still under it for a long time, gradually feeling warmth seep into her chilled body. Finally she stepped from the shower stall and dried off briskly. Her hair was hopeless; the only thing she could do was wrap it in a towel.

She pulled Adam's robe from its hook and shrugged into it, then stared into the fogged mirror. She was fairly lost in the folds of extra fabric. She rolled the sleeves up, drew the lapels together, tightened the belt, and looked again. Not much better, but it would have to do. With a sigh she opened the bathroom door and went out into the bedroom.

She walked barefoot across the room to the door and opened it. The hallway was empty; a faint light showed from the living room. She found the living room empty, too, and made her way to the kitchen.

Adam, with his shirt sleeves rolled up, stood before the stove, ladling soup into two bowls. He placed the pot back on the burner and then turned, freezing when he saw her standing in the doorway. His black eyes moved slowly over her, brooding, unreadable.

Adam drew in his breath sharply and turned away from her, almost as though he could no longer bear to look at her. "Sit down," he said brusquely, gesturing toward the small table in the corner of the room. Silently Heather did as he asked.

The meal was a quiet one; neither of them had very much to say. Tension stretched between them, as it always did whenever the two of them were alone. Heather felt his eyes on her from time to time, but when she glanced up, he was always paying attention to his food.

When she had finished, Heather rose and started to carry her bowl to the sink, but Adam stopped her with an abrupt gesture. "I'll do that. You shouldn't walk around with wet hair. There's a dryer in the top lefthand drawer of my dresser."

Convinced that he wanted her out of his apartment as soon as possible, Heather felt tears come to her eyes. Quickly, before he could notice, she turned and left the room, almost running.

In his bedroom she found the dryer and quickly dried her hair, standing by the dresser. She didn't look at her reflection in the mirror; she didn't want to see the pain she felt shining in her eyes. When her hair was dry, she turned off the dryer and set it on the dresser, and then looked up to meet Adam's brooding eyes in the mirror. He was standing just behind her, and she felt almost hypnotized by the intensity of his eyes.

He reached up slowly to smooth her hair, staring at the reflection in the mirror of the small bruise on her arm. "Did I do that?"

Heather nodded mutely, her breath catching when he bent forward to press his lips briefly to the bruise.

When he straightened, there was a faint, mocking smile curving his lips. "There. All better now?"

She turned suddenly, staring up at him with darkly purple eyes. "I'm not a child."

His smile disappeared, the black eyes kindled with fiery desire. "Don't start something if you don't mean to go through with it," he said roughly. "I can't take that again, Heather. Once I touch you, I won't be able to stop. Not this time."

"No, not this time, Adam." As easily as that, she had made her decision. She gazed up at him, purple eyes filled with helpless need.

"Tell me what you want," he commanded, a low, driven note in his voice. "Tell me, Heather."

"I—I want . . . you."

And then she was in his arms, his lips capturing hers with a hungry demand that shook her to her roots. Having

142

burned all her bridges, Heather made no attempt to temper her own response. Her arms slipped around his neck, her fingers tangling in his hair as her mouth opened willingly, eagerly beneath his.

She lowered her arms only to slip them from the sleeves of the robe as he pushed it off her shoulders, her fingers immediately searching out the buttons of his shirt. No qualms held her back this time when she touched the silver medallion around his neck. She wanted to belong to him, and that primitive need, acknowledged and accepted, drove every other thought from her mind.

In moments they were on the bed, the room lit only by the soft golden glow of the lamp on the nightstand.

Heather had never dreamed that a man could be so strong and yet so tender. Powerful, sensitive hands moved over her body with butterfly softness, caressing, cherishing, loving. With a delicate touch he seemed to try to memorize her body, imprint it on his hands for all time.

With less experience, but with the same burning desire driving her, Heather explored his body, feeling a sudden surge of power when he trembled beneath her hands. She wanted to go on touching him forever, but the spiraling tension within her demanded a satisfaction that could not be achieved by mere touch. Shifting restlessly, she moaned softly, "Take me, Adam, please."

He moved over her, breathing deeply, harshly. "Sweet Heather," he murmured unsteadily. "Oh, *God*, I need you, darling!"

The universe receded, time ground to a halt. Vaguely Heather thought that they had even stopped breathing, but it didn't seem important. Violet eyes, black eyes, locked in wordless communication. During the seconds, the eternities which passed, Heather felt that she was gazing into him, past the obsidian pools of his eyes, into his very soul. A sense of wonder filled her, a curious

143

feeling of completion, as though she had suddenly found the half of herself she had not known was missing.

Two minds seemed to mesh, two hearts beat as one. And then their bodies moved slowly, dreamlike, to make the joining physical as well as mental.

It was unlike anything Heather had ever experienced, a pleasure she had not dreamed was possible. The tension within her grew and grew, filling her body, her mind, her senses. And then she was flying, soaring, calling out Adam's name as rapture pierced her body, dimly aware of him groaning out her own name.

Sanity returned slowly to Heather. She lay enfolded in Adam's arms, only half aware when he drew the covers up around them and pressed his lips briefly to her forehead. Dreamily she listened to his heart beating beneath her cheek, untroubled by thought. Pleasantly exhausted, she finally drifted off to sleep.

It was several hours later when she woke, her eyes snapping open abruptly, as if from a nightmare. And it had been a nightmare. She had been walking with Adam through a shaded forest, happy, content. And then, quite suddenly, a man had stepped from the trees in front of them, his face indistinguishable in the shadows. Adam had turned accusing eyes to her, then shook off the pleading hand on his arm and walked away, disappearing through the trees. She had been alone in the forest with a man who had no face.

Now, trembling, she moved cautiously from the arms holding her loosely until she was sitting on the edge of the bed. She was bewildered and frightened. She had never felt so alone in her life. The dream had forced her to face reality, a reality she had avoided even after Adam's possession had shown her the truth.

The faceless man of her dream was the equally faceless man in her past. The knowledge was inescapable, unavoidable. And he was real. She knew that now. Because she had not been a virgin.

Did Adam know? She stared down at his face, relaxed, oddly vulnerable in sleep. Was it true that a man couldn't be sure about these things? Or perhaps he did know and simply hadn't cared. He had made no declaration of love, after all. No commitment.

But she cared. Sometime during the lost six months of her life she had loved a man enough to give herself to him. It was said that a woman never forgot her first lover. Why had she forgotten hers? What in God's name had happened during that six months?

And whom had she betrayed on this night? Had she betrayed Adam by allowing him to believe that she was free to love him? Had she betrayed that other man by loving Adam when she had no right to? Or had she betrayed herself by loving one man with the memory of another locked away and hidden in her heart?

She stared down at Adam, knowing that she loved him, knowing that she would take whatever he could give her, even if it was only a brief affair. But did she have the right to even that? Adam cared about her, she knew. He could not have made love to her with such tenderness if he had wanted only to possess her. She did not know how much he cared, or how long he would care. Could he learn to love her as she loved him?

What if he asked her to live with him, perhaps even to marry him? How could she commit herself to him with the shadow of another man between them?

She could not. It was a tormenting decision to make, bringing tears to Heather's bitter, pain-laden eyes, but it was unavoidable. Until she had faced her past, she could not look to the future. No matter what Adam wanted of her, whether it was a brief affair or a lifetime commitment, she had to find out about that other man.

Adam shifted restively, turning his face into the pillow

beside his own, murmuring her name almost inaudibly. The quiet sound set the seal on Heather's decision, and she slipped from the bed and went into the bathroom to dress. She knew that he would not understand her leaving without a word, would be angry, but she couldn't remain to face him. What could she say? That she had to find the man in her past? She could imagine how he would react to that!

No, it was better this way. But, God, how she hated leaving him! He made her feel alive, complete for the first time in her life. She loved him, wanted to spend the rest of her life with him. If only she could ignore the shadowy existence of that other man. But she couldn't. Not now.

She went back through the bedroom, picking up her purse and pausing for a last glance at the man sleeping in the bed, then she hurried from the room. Silently she moved through the quiet apartment, stopping only when she reached the door to the spare room, halfway down the long hall. For some reason she felt drawn to that room, as if something within beckoned to her.

Like one in a dream, she stepped over to the door, watching, in a detached manner, as her hand reached out to try the knob. Unlocked. Before she could change her mind, she stepped into the darkened room and closed the door. Then, steeling herself against she knew not what, she flipped up the light switch. And in the eternal moment after light flooded the room, she remembered what she had once told Leon about her inability to remember, comparing her reluctance to being in an unfamiliar room in total darkness and not knowing what she would see when the lights came on.

This room was eerily like the one she had alluded to. In fact, it *was* that room. The locked room in her mind.

But it was unlocked now. And now she knew why she had been so strongly attracted to Adam, why she had been

146

unable to resist him. Now she knew why she had responded to him when no other man had the power to move her.

The room was a studio, an artist's studio. It smelled of oil paints and turpentine and bore a cluttered appearance. A large worktable held tubes of paints and cans of brushes. Canvases, finished and unfinished, were stacked against the wall on the left. But it was the right side of the room that held Heather's stunned gaze.

Two canvases reposed on easels, side by side, one finished, one incomplete. The one on the left was the painting of herself that Leon had taken her to see. The second painting was one she had never seen, but the subject was the same: herself.

The background had not been filled in, or even sketched, but her face and figure had been captured with the same amazing skill of the first portrait. She was sitting with hands folded in her lap, dressed severely in black, her hair drawn back in a smooth chignon. But where the first portrait had been of a girl filled with love and laughter, this second one was of a woman with strange other-world eyes, eyes shadowed and haunted by a pain she would not let herself remember. A pain buried so deeply, hidden so completely, that it took the shock of this moment to retrieve it from the black void where her wounded mind had placed it three years before.

Hyde. God, why hadn't she seen it sooner? *Hyde:* an alter ego, a dual personality.

Adam Blake, businessman, head of two prominent firms on both the East and West Coasts, wealthy, powerful. Adam Blake, gifted, sensitive artist, driven by his talent, torn by the necessity that had forced him to live in the commercial world of advertising.

Adam, a man who felt with the depth and perception of the truly gifted, whose clarity of mind was sometimes astounding and always a lodestar to a troubled friend, whose strength of character had carried him through the long, wasted years after a father's selfish desires had forced him to hide his God-given ability.

Adam, the man she had fallen in love with three and a half years ago, the man she had married, the man whose child she had carried briefly, so briefly, before losing it in an accident that should never have happened . . .

The door was unlocked, finally and completely. With a strangled whimper like that of a wounded animal, Heather sank down to her knees on the carpet. It hurt unbearably to breathe, white-hot irons piercing her lungs with every shuddering gasp. Her mind forced her to remember, mercilessly recounting every moment of those months.

The brief courtship filled with strain because—she saw now—of her youth and uncertainty. Adam's insistence that they marry and, again, her uncertainty. Her first meeting with Daniel Blake, fraught with hostility on his side and near terror on hers. The passionate months alone with Adam after their quiet marriage. Her final confrontation with Daniel when Adam had been absent from their home and she had come rushing in bursting with the news of her pregnancy. Daniel's scornful, cruel presentation of divorce papers, and her agonized flight.

It all came back. All of it. Her car skidding on the slippery road, the sickening sound of crumpling metal and shattering glass. The confused blur of pain and bright lights, the whispered, desperate plea concerning her baby and the answer that had sent her mind retreating in torment from one blow too many. And later, vaguely, the muted conversations of doctors. Such a pity; she was so young. But she could always adopt, of course.

Tears rolling down her white cheeks, Heather hugged herself with trembling arms. "Oh, God, Daniel," she whispered raggedly, "because of you, I've lost him twice!"

She stumbled to her feet and left the room, turning off the light and closing the door automatically. As she opened the front door and slipped through, she heard

Adam calling "Heather? *Heather!*" and the anxiety and alarm in his voice tore at her. Quickly, quietly, she closed the door and hurried to the elevator.

Once outside the building, she walked quickly away from Adam's apartment, away from the apartment she shared with Lisa. When she was far enough away to feel safe, her steps slowed.

Everything should have been so simple. The return of her memory had brought the knowledge that Adam was the only man in her life, and that should have made the whole bewildering situation all right. She should have been able to go back and talk to him, discuss what had happened three years ago, find out why he had not told her who he was and who she was when he had come to San Francisco.

But she didn't need to ask Adam those questions. She had gotten to know him during these last weeks, and she understood him far better than she had during their short marriage. This time she had been a mature woman, capable of seeing him clearly, not intimidated by Daniel's violent disapproval, not made to feel inadequate by her own inexperience.

Adam would not have left his father to break the news of a divorce. He was not a coward. The divorce had been a deception of Daniel's. Daniel, who had been furious when his son turned away from him and the family business to marry a nobody and pursue the art he loved. He had blamed Heather for that, and he had been determined to break them up. And his deception had worked, because Heather had been too young emotionally to understand the complex personality of her husband.

As for Adam's silence on the subject of their marriage, that, too, was easily explained. He had simply not wanted to shock her by the revelation, realizing that she would have to remember in her own time, in her own way.

Heather glanced around suddenly to find herself in the

children's park again, and her heart lurched in pain as she stared at the tiny rides and fountains. It should have been so simple . . . but it wasn't.

She couldn't go back to Adam. She couldn't live with him as his wife. She felt that he loved her, knew that she loved him. But she couldn't remain his wife knowing that she could never give him a child. Oh, he would say that it didn't matter. He was that kind of man.

But it mattered. Adam loved children, and he had always wanted a large family. They both had. She an only child, and he from a broken home . . . And Heather ached inside now for the child she had lost, the children that would never be.

And she hated Daniel Blake, bitterly, painfully.

She neither knew nor cared where her footsteps led, but continued to walk aimlessly. It was hours later when she suddenly realized that she was standing in front of her apartment building. The sun had risen; birds chirped merrily in the early morning quiet.

Heather studied the parking lot for a long moment, but no silver-gray Mercedes revealed itself to her searching gaze. She let herself into the building and went up to her apartment. As she closed the door behind her, Lisa emerged from the kitchen, fully dressed and obviously worried.

"Thank God!" she exclaimed in relief. "Heather, where on earth have you been? We've been worried to death!"

"We?" Heather dropped her purse on the coffee table and sank wearily into a chair.

"Yes, *we!*" Lisa collapsed on the couch, drawing her jean-clad legs beneath her. "I called Daddy after Adam woke me up banging on the door at three A.M."

Heather frowned slightly, not really surprised that Adam had come looking for her. "You shouldn't have called Leon," she murmured.

"Well, what was I supposed to do? There was Adam,

pacing around the apartment like a man demented, throwing cryptic comments all over the place."

"Cryptic comments?"

Lisa sighed impatiently. "Yes. He said something about you running out on him again, and that this time he wasn't going to let you get away. He was in no mood to explain, and I was too confused to ask. So I called Daddy, and as soon as he got here, he started roaring at Adam."

"Roaring?" Heather's eyes widened in surprise. "Leon?"

"It surprised me too," Lisa murmured. "I've never seen Daddy so upset. He told Adam that it was all his fault, and that the last time you'd run away from him, something dreadful had happened. More cryptic comments." She paused and looked quizzically at her friend. "I didn't realize they knew each other."

"Do they?" Heather shrugged wearily. "I've never heard either of them mention it if they do."

Lisa grimaced slightly. "Well, if they don't, then they certainly conceived an immediate and mutual hostility. I've never heard such language! Anyway, they stood there, yelling at each other and not making very much sense. When it looked like they were going to start slugging it out, I stepped in and reminded them that you were still among the missing. That quieted them, and they left to try and find you."

"Together?"

"Hardly." She grimaced again. "They split up outside, each taking a different section of the city." Lisa grinned suddenly. "You should feel honored—not to mention medieval—to have two handsome men fighting over you. Or about you. Whatever."

Heather managed a slight smile, but shook her head. "I'm too confused to feel honored."

"*You're* confused!" Lisa rolled her eyes toward heaven in exasperation. "I'll admit that when you didn't come

151

home last night, I figured you were with Adam, which didn't really surprise me. But after he barged in here, nothing made any sense. What happened last night, Heather?"

After a moment, Heather said slowly, "It's a long story, Lisa, and I really don't feel up to telling it right now. I'll tell you all about it later." She rose to her feet and started for her room. "I have to get away for a while."

"Heather, I don't think you should," Lisa objected worriedly, following her friend into the bedroom. "Daddy will kill me if I let you run off. What am I saying? *Adam* will kill me. Besides," she went on with brutal frankness, "you look like hell."

"Thanks," Heather returned dryly, taking a suitcase from the closet and opening it on the bed.

Lisa leaned against the doorjamb and glared at her irritably. "Well, you do! You're white as a sheet and obviously exhausted. You're in no shape to be going—where are you going anyway?"

Heather, rapidly packing the suitcase, shook her head vaguely. "I don't know. Just somewhere. I have to think."

"Oh, great!" Lisa exclaimed sarcastically. "Is that what I'm supposed to tell Daddy and Adam? That you've just gone off into the wild blue yonder and I have no idea where? Not bloody likely!"

Heather straightened after closing the case and regarded her friend with a faint sigh. "Lisa, I'm not suicidal. I'm not going to get behind the wheel of a car or swallow a handful of pills. And I'm not running away from anything. I'm facing something. But I have to face it alone." She smiled crookedly. "I'll be back. Tell them that. A few days, a week. I'll be back."

Lisa continued to object. In fact, she was still objecting when Heather firmly closed the apartment door. For all the good it did her.

Heather had no definite plan in mind. She just wanted

to find a quiet place and spend a few days alone. It disturbed her to know that Adam would be worried by her absence, but she couldn't face him yet. Not until she found some way of facing everything she had remembered.

Her steps led her, oddly enough, toward the bay. She stood and stared out over the water for a long moment, until a masculine voice from behind her caused her to start in surprise.

"Heather?"

She turned to find James Norden standing on the path that led up to the street, frowning at her. "I thought that was you. Is anything wrong?" His glance dropped to the suitcase at her feet.

Heather managed a faint smile. "Hello, James. No, nothing's wrong. I wasn't planning on going for a swim, if that's what you were thinking."

"How about a sink?" He looked at her gravely. "You look pretty distraught."

She laughed involuntarily. "No, not a sink either. I was just trying to think of someplace where I could spend a few days or a week and think things out."

He pursed his lips thoughtfully for a moment, and then came over and bent to pick up her suitcase. "I know the perfect place. It's quiet, private, and no telephones to bother you. You can stay as long as you like."

Heather looked puzzled. "It sounds perfect, but where is it?"

"Two-thirty-four Oak Street," he replied cheerfully, taking her by the arm and leading her up the path.

"But that's your address! I can't—"

"Sure you can. Margie and I are leaving in a couple of hours for a cruise. We'll be gone for two months, and the house'll be completely empty. Stay as long as you like."

As they emerged onto the street, Heather saw with surprise that it was his neighborhood. Accurately reading her look, Norden said calmly, "I always go down to the bay in the morning and watch the boats on the water. It's good exercise—the walk, that is. I never expected to see you there."

"James, thank you for the offer, but I really couldn't—"

"Of course you can. And you will. You'll be doing me a favor, Heather, really. I don't want to leave the house empty."

"But—"

"There's an answering service to take calls, so you won't be bothered," he cut her off cheerfully. "You can still call out if you want, but you won't be disturbed. It's a quiet neighborhood. When you decide to leave, just drop the key off with my next-door neighbor, and he'll watch the house until we get back."

Weakening, Heather murmured, "I don't want to impose."

He grinned slightly. "You aren't. I'd rather have you in the house than a stranger any day. I've trusted you with my reputation more than once. I'm sure I can trust you with the family silver."

Warmed by his trust and concern, Heather gave in. As he had intended her to all along.

CHAPTER NINE

Several weeks passed, and Heather was no nearer to a solution than she had been that first day. She ached to see Adam, to hear his voice, but she dared not go near him. He would convince her that a child of their own was not that important to him, that they could always adopt, and she would give in to him.

It was something she couldn't do. No matter what he said, it simply wouldn't be fair to him. Not since she knew how much having children meant to him. She loved him too much.

She lost weight she could ill-afford to lose, eating very little and walking a great deal. Every morning she walked down to the bay to watch the boats—just as Norden had—finding an odd peace in the sight. Sometimes she stayed for hours.

On this particular Thursday, she had just returned from the bay when the doorbell rang. Puzzled, she opened the door and it was hard to say who was more shocked, she or her unexpected guest.

"Heather!"

Daniel Blake was an older edition of his son physically.

The black hair was heavily frosted with silver, the thin face deeply tanned and lined with nearly sixty years of hard living. The same unfathomable black eyes gleamed like jet beneath flying brows, and he was every bit as tall and broad-shouldered as his son. He was, however, much thinner than she remembered, and his face seemed almost wasted. But the greatest change of all was the absence of his wheelchair. He was standing.

"May I come in, Heather? I'd like to talk to you." He seemed hesitant, unsure of his welcome, as well he might be.

She hesitated for a moment and then stepped back and gestured for him to enter. Closing the door behind him, she led the way into the living room and turned to face him. "What do you want, Daniel?" she asked quietly.

His thin lips twisted slightly. "D'you mind if I sit down? If I stand too long, my back'll give me hell tomorrow."

Without comment she motioned him toward a chair and then sat down across from it. Daniel sank down a bit awkwardly, his taut face relaxing as the weight was removed from his legs. He studied Heather's calm expression for a long moment, then said abruptly, "I saw your name on a computer printout of Norden employees last week. It wasn't until then that I realized why Adam had been so determined to buy the company."

Disregarding this, she asked curiously, "How did you know where to find me?"

"I didn't." He shrugged. "I went to your apartment and talked to your roommate. She's very worried about you, by the way. Then I decided to contact Norden, thinking that he might know where you were. The answering service said that he was out of town, but I took a chance and came by anyway. It was—a bit of a shock finding you here."

"You haven't been in touch with Adam?"

"No," he answered heavily. "I haven't spoken to my

son directly for more than two years, Heather. After I . . . after you left, he spent six months looking for you. Then I had a mild heart attack, and he came back to New York and took over the company again." Daniel's mouth thinned bitterly. "He said he didn't want my death on his conscience, that he'd run the business until David was old enough to take over. He hates me for what I did to the two of you." With a slight shake of his head, he went on harshly. "God knows you should hate me, too, Heather, but you don't, do you?"

"I should hate you," Heather said frankly. "If I'd had three years to brood, I *would* hate you—bitterly. But there was an accident the night after I left Adam, and I lost my memory. Until a few weeks ago I didn't remember you— or Adam. When I remembered, I hated you . . . for a while."

"An accident?" Daniel's face slowly whitened. "Were you—badly hurt, Heather?"

She stared at him for a long moment, suddenly realizing that she felt no desire for revenge. Daniel had acted wrongly three years before, and he had paid for that mistake with the loss of his son. Gazing at the face that was marked with lines of pain and bitterness, seeing the anxiety in his eyes, she knew that it would destroy him to find out exactly what his cruel deception had cost her—and him. And she couldn't tell him. He was an arrogant old tyrant, but he loved his son and she knew it.

Quietly she said, "No, Daniel. I wasn't badly hurt," and trusted that God would forgive the lie.

Daniel looked relieved and dropped his gaze to the tightly clasped hands in his lap. "I'm glad," he muttered gruffly. "I never meant to hurt you. I know you don't believe that, but it's the truth. You were barely out of your teens; Adam was twelve years older. The two of you were from different worlds. I thought that you were just infatuated with Adam, that you'd soon get over him."

"And Adam?" With an effort, Heather kept her voice even. "How did you explain away his feelings?"

Daniel winced slightly and shook his head. "I thought that Adam was infatuated as well. It seemed likely. You were so completely different from the women he'd known before, and you were encouraging him . . ." His voice trailed away.

Quietly Heather finished the sentence. "To paint. Is that why you decided to break us up, because I encouraged Adam to go against your wishes?"

His face sagging abruptly, Daniel looked up at her with an expression of humility in his eyes. "I'm sorry, Heather," he said simply. "I was wrong. I suppose I knew it even then."

Heather sighed tiredly. "It was Adam's decision, Daniel, not mine. He said that he was tired of that kind of life, that he wanted to spend his time painting and . . . and being with me. I didn't realize that his art had been a bone of contention between you for years."

"All his life," Daniel muttered, his gaze falling once again to his clasped hands. "We got along like two cats tied up in a bag, he and I. Because we were always so different, I suppose. I never liked art, never understood it. God knows where Adam got his talent."

A faint, rueful twinkle flickered in Heather's violet eyes for a moment. "At least you can admit now that he *has* talent; three years ago, you wouldn't even go that far."

There was a moment of silence, and then Daniel looked up at his daughter-in-law, his dark eyes oddly opaque. "Three years ago," he said quietly, "Adam came home to that cottage and found me there and you gone. He came in and saw the phony divorce papers, and your rings on the floor where you'd thrown them. And he looked at me with real hate in his eyes."

Heather hastily averted her gaze from the pain shining in the dark eyes that were so like Adam's. "I shouldn't

158

have run away. If I had understood Adam better, I wouldn't have run." Her voice was low and haunted as she thought of everything she'd lost by that foolish, blind action. "I believed you when you told me that Adam had never really loved me . . . and I ran."

"He loved you," Daniel said gently. "I never realized how much until I saw his face when he went charging out to search for you that night. It was like he'd just lost the one thing he cherished more than anything else in the world." He sighed heavily. "I realized then what I'd done, and I prayed that he'd find you. I even hired detectives myself, but they couldn't discover a trace of you."

For the first time, Heather looked faintly skeptical. "You wanted him to find me? Then why, when Adam came back to New York, did you shout at him about ruining his life over some little tramp?"

Daniel frowned. "Did Adam tell you that?"

"No. Someone who was in the building at the time."

Still frowning, he said, "It isn't true. Oh, we were both yelling, and I did tell him that he was ruining his health— he looked like he'd been dragged through the desert at the end of a thorny rope—but I didn't say anything derogatory about you. At that point, Heather, I would have given everything I owned to see you walk through the door."

Heather believed him. It went against everything she had ever heard or known about him, but she knew that he was speaking the truth. Adam had always loved and respected his father, even though, as Daniel had remarked, they had fought like cats in a bag. But Daniel had meddled just once too often in his son's life, and his actions had destroyed the bond between them. It was that which had changed Daniel, had made a different man of him.

With a slight grimace Daniel muttered, "Adam was doing most of the shouting. He wasn't in a very forgiving mood. I couldn't blame him. He'd just spent more than six months trying to find you, and he didn't even know if you were dead or alive. That's when he told me that he was resuming control of the company because he didn't want my death on his conscience and for no other reason, and that he'd stay only until David was old enough to take over. Then he said that he hoped the next time he saw me, it would be in hell."

Troubled, Heather said, "That doesn't sound like Adam. No matter what you'd done, you're still his father!"

With a sigh Daniel shook his head. "He had every right to talk to me that way. All his life I'd played God, tried to bend Adam to my will, tried to mold him into something he wasn't. I knew damn well he wasn't happy in the business world, but that's where I wanted him, and that's where I forced him to be. He wanted no part of the company, flatly refused to take over his last year in college. Then I had that accident, and I took full advantage of the fact that I was confined to a wheelchair." The dark eyes flashed in self-contempt. "Emotional blackmail!"

"You made the accident seem worse than it actually was?" she asked uncertainly.

Daniel shrugged. "If you mean could I have run the company from the wheelchair, yes, I could have. And the doctors told me a few months after the accident that there was an operation that would give me an eighty percent chance of walking as well as I ever had. Needless to say, I never told Adam that. I let him think that I was only a broken old man, permanently tied to a wheelchair and only kept alive by that bloody company."

He looked up to see her shocked face, and his own face twisted bitterly. "I know. It was a rotten, despicable thing to do. But I believed that the end justified the means, and since Adam was running the business, I was satisfied. He was doing better with it than I ever had, and I convinced myself that I'd been right all along: Adam was a businessman, not an artist. I thought that he'd forgotten all about his painting—which shows how well I knew my son! He's been painting all along, hasn't he, Heather?"

Heather nodded slowly, staring down at her hands. "All along. He signed his paintings Hyde, because he didn't want to cause trouble between you. But even with the pseudonym, he didn't exhibit any of his paintings."

The lines of pain in Daniel's face deepened. "I stole that from him as well as everything else, didn't I? The recognition that should have been his all these years."

She looked up at him with a faint, disturbed frown on her face. "You still don't understand, Daniel. Adam never painted hoping to become famous. He painted because . . . because it was in him to paint. It's his way of dealing with himself. He paints his thoughts and his feelings. If he's moved or troubled by something, he puts it on canvas."

Daniel sighed softly. "And he hid that from me all these years, because he knew that I wouldn't understand. And he was right. I didn't understand. I was furious when he met you and announced that he was leaving the company for good. Maybe he'd begun to suspect that I wasn't as helpless as I pretended, I don't know. Anyway, he told me that he was through, and I tried to play God again. I deliberately destroyed his marriage to you and he hates me for that."

After a moment, Heather asked quietly, "When did you have the operation?"

Slowly Daniel said, "A few months ago I went to Adam's apartment in New York. I knew he was at a board meeting and I . . ." He shifted uncomfortably. "Oh, hell, I wanted to see how he was living. Since you'd run away, he had been acting like a hermit. I was worried about him. Douglas let me in, even though I'm sure he had orders not to, and I spent an hour or so just looking around." With a weary shake of his head, he muttered, "Most of the rooms were empty of personality, as if no one lived there.

161

There was no trace of Adam at all, except in the study. Douglas showed it to me, said that Adam spent most of his time in there alone."

There was an odd expression on Daniel's face. Very quietly he went on. "But I don't think he was ever alone in there, Heather, not really. There was a portrait set up on an easel in front of a chair. A portrait of you."

Heather stared at him fixedly, thinking of Adam alone in that room night after night, gazing at the portrait he had painted of the wife he had lost, and her heart moved suddenly, painfully, inside her.

Apparently not noticing her reaction, Daniel said, "That decided me to have the operation. The only thing Adam wanted from me was his freedom, and I knew I had to give it to him."

Pushing the desolate image from her mind, Heather asked unsteadily, "Does Adam know that you can walk?"

Daniel shook his head. "I doubt it. I kept the operation quiet until I knew for certain that it was a success. That was several weeks ago, and that was when Adam pitched everything into David's lap and came out here. I was baffled until I saw your name on the list of Norden employees." He stared at her intently. "I thought . . . I hoped that you and Adam would be back together by now. Your roommate said that there had been some sort of fight between you two. What happened, Heather?"

"Lisa said that?" Heather frowned slightly, ignoring his quiet question. "That's not like her. Unless . . ." She stared at him in dawning suspicion.

Daniel smiled slightly as he read the accusing question in her expressive eyes. "Guilty. I'm sorry, Heather, but I knew nothing about your memory loss. I told Lisa that I was your father-in-law."

Wryly Heather asked, "How did she take it?"

A flicker of amusement showed briefly in his dark eyes. "She seemed more satisfied than surprised." He hesitated, then said very quietly, "You didn't answer my question, Heather."

Absently Heather twisted the bracelet on her left wrist —the bracelet that Adam had given her shortly after their marriage. She looked up to see the anxiety on Daniel's face, and smiled slightly. "What happened . . . happened only in my mind, I think."

"You're going back to Adam?" he asked quickly.

Heather dropped her eyes to the bracelet. "If he'll have me." She looked up in time to catch his expression of relief, and her smile widened. "And I think he will."

"I know he will!" His grin faded quickly, replaced with a very serious expression. "I don't expect you to forgive me, Heather, but I hope you believe how sorry I am about what I did to you and Adam."

"I believe you." Heather got to her feet and watched as he did the same. "And I forgive you." He looked startled, and Heather went on quietly. "I think that Adam will forgive you, too, one day."

"Thank you, Heather," Daniel murmured almost inaudibly. "That means more than I can say."

Feeling suddenly lighthearted, Heather said teasingly, "They say that a leopard can't change its spots. But if you ever decide to change yours back, Daniel, be warned! You won't be dealing with an uncertain young girl this time, and I'll fight for what's mine!"

Perhaps realizing that she was speaking only partly in jest, he smiled faintly and said, "I'm not a big enough fool to make the same mistake twice, Heather, believe me. I'll never try to meddle in Adam's life again."

Heather laughed softly as she accompanied him to the door. "Will David take over the company?"

"If he wants to."

"And if he doesn't?" she smiled.

Daniel stood in the open doorway and looked down at

his daughter-in-law with a rueful smile. "Then he won't. I *have* learned my lesson, Heather."

Impulsively Heather hugged him, secretly amused when he looked nonplussed. "Thank you, Daniel." She stepped back to smile at him.

"For what?" he asked in surprise.

Still lighthearted, Heather shrugged. "Oh, I was at a fork in the road and didn't know which way to go. Thanks to you, I know now."

"The road that leads to Adam?" he asked seriously.

She nodded. "The road that leads to Adam. I never should have strayed from it. And I won't stray again."

A little puzzled, but obviously relieved, Daniel nodded and stepped off the porch. Then he hesitated and looked back at her. "If—if you're ever in New York, Heather . . ." he began gruffly, and then shrugged. "The house has seemed awfully empty these last few years. I'd welcome a little company."

Softly Heather asked, "May I bring a friend?"

He looked at once hopeful and uncertain. "Do you really think that he would?"

"I think that he would."

Clearly struggling beneath the powerful weight of his emotions, Daniel managed to say roughly, "Any friend of yours . . ." and then he turned toward his car.

Heather stood in the doorway and watched until his car disappeared. She went into the house, her mind clear for the first time in weeks. God, what a fool she had been! A selfish fool. All this time she had been thinking of how her decision would affect her, but she had never once stopped to think of how it would affect Adam. What right did she have to make a decision that would affect, not only her life, but his as well?

Her thanks to Daniel had been sincere. His visit had shown her plainly the hell that Adam had lived in for three years. She herself had been protected from the pain of their parting by her memory loss, but Adam had possessed no such shield. All this time he had stared at a painting and asked himself where she was and if she was all right with no certainty that she was even alive.

And he was going through the same thing right now! She glanced at a calendar on the wall and then reached for the phone. Six weeks! For six weeks she had tried to convince herself that she alone had the right to decide the future course of their marriage, while Adam waited and wondered. God, she was cruel!

Suddenly her hand froze, and startled eyes returned to the calendar. Six weeks? Almost numbly her mind calculated dates and events. No, no, it wasn't possible! *Was it?*

It was nerves, tension. She repeated the thought like a talisman to ward off certain disappointment as she reached for the phone book and hastily looked up the number of a nearby doctor. It was difficult to arrange an appointment on such short notice, but her determination would brook no interference. She got the appointment.

Moments later she was snatching up her purse and hurrying from the house, telling herself fiercely that she mustn't hope too much. It would only hurt more when . . .

Late that afternoon Heather found herself wandering in the general direction of her apartment. The realization snapped her mind from its dreamy state, and her footsteps suddenly became brisk. First she had to talk to Leon.

She let herself into the apartment quietly. A glance at her watch told her that Lisa should still be at work, but some instinct said that the apartment would not be empty. Closing the door behind her, she looked across the room to see Leon sitting on the couch.

He was watching a news program on television, but looked up as he heard the soft click of the door closing. Immediately he used the remote control to switch off the set and then slumped slightly and passed a weary hand over his face. "Thank God," he muttered. "I was beginning to think . . ." His voice trailed off as he looked across the room at her with grim eyes.

"That I'd had another accident?" Heather came farther into the room and sat down on the chair beside the couch. "I'm sorry, Leon. I should have let all of you know that I was all right. I just lost track of the time."

"Where have you been, Heather?"

She shrugged. "Norden's house. He and his wife have gone out of town for a couple of months, and he told me that I could stay there as long as I wanted to."

Leon sighed. "Couldn't you have called? We . . ." He grimaced slightly. "*All* of us would have felt much better just knowing that you were still in San Francisco."

Gently Heather said, "I had to think, Leon."

He seemed about to protest and then nodded slightly. Looking at her intently, he said, "You've remembered."

She nodded. "Everything."

His gaze dropped to his hands. He was silent for a long moment. "Heather, there are a few things I have to tell you."

Unwilling to cause him any more pain than she had already, she said quickly, "Leon, you really don't have to say anything."

"Yes." He looked across at her, his expression a little wry. "I do, Heather."

Realizing that he felt compelled to get everything out of his system, Heather inclined her head slightly and waited to hear what he had to say.

He returned his gaze to his hands. "When they wheeled you out of the operating room three years ago, I had already read the police report. I knew that there was no one, apparently, to take care of you. I saw you open your eyes and ask that stupidly insensitive nurse a question, and before I could stop her, she answered you. I saw the agony

166

in your eyes and I knew that I couldn't just walk away from you."

He smiled faintly, sadly. "You were so very alone, all covered in bandages, with casts on an arm and a leg. I knew that you wouldn't be scarred, except for that one tiny cut, but I wanted to take care of you. So I took you to Colorado."

Heather stared at him. "You knew about . . . about my . . ."

"About your baby?" He nodded. "At first I believed that it was the loss of your baby that you couldn't bear to remember. But then the months went by, and that six months remained a blank to you. That's when I realized that there was much more involved.

"I had spent enough time talking to you to understand what kind of person you were. I knew that you must have loved the father of your child very much. Whether he had been your lover or your husband, I didn't know. But I knew that he mattered to you, mattered so much that you couldn't bear to remember him."

He looked up at her with a rueful smile. "I told myself that in time you'd get over that man. That one day you'd remember him and feel no pain, and he'd be gone from your heart. Then the months turned into years, and I knew it wouldn't happen. I started to believe, then, that I would never be able to make you happy. It wasn't any fault of yours or mine, it was just that you'd already given everything you had to give. That man locked away inside your mind, he had it all. Whether he wanted it or not.

"And then I saw the painting. Everything about that painting, every brushstroke, every tiny detail, spoke of love. The man who had painted that portrait loved you with everything inside of him, and I knew that. He had to be the man in your past, and whatever had split the two of you up, it wasn't a lack of love."

Quietly Heather said, "That's why you took me to see the portrait."

He nodded. "When you reacted the way you did, I knew that I had been right." He looked at her with a faint sigh. "Lisa told me that Daniel Blake was here this morning. That just confirmed what I'd already guessed."

Heather smiled slightly. "Hyde," she murmured.

Leon's response was a faintly crooked grin. "Hyde. Meaning: another self."

"Two halves of the same person." Heather sighed softly. "It was sort of an ironic joke."

Leon nodded silently, and the room was quiet for a long moment. Then he stared across at Heather levelly. "I want you to understand something. I loved Lisa's mother very much, and when she died, I didn't think I'd ever love again. And then you came along, and I knew I had been wrong. I'm grateful for that, Heather. Some men go through their entire lives without finding one woman they can love; I found two." Amusement entered his eyes. "I don't promise that I'll start thinking of you as another daughter, but I will get over you, Heather. I've been getting over you since I first saw that painting."

Heather smiled shakily, her eyes filling with tears. "Thank you, Leon, for understanding. I never wanted to hurt you."

Very quietly Leon said, "I don't have the memories that Adam has, Heather. Memories of holding you in my arms all night. That's the kind of thing a man never gets over."

Before Heather could respond, there was a rattle of keys in the front door and Lisa came into the apartment. Immediately she rushed across the room to hug Heather and then collapsed on the coffee table. "Thank God you're home! I was beginning to think of myself as a liar every time I promised Adam you'd come back."

Heather flushed softly. "How is he?" When Lisa looked

at her uncertainly, she laughed. "It's okay, Lisa, I remember everything."

Lisa sighed with relief. "Good. I was afraid I'd have to tiptoe around the subject, and God knows I'm no ballerina!"

"We know!" Leon chuckled. "Now tell Heather how that husband of hers is before she has a fit."

Sensing that her father and her best friend had talked things out and reached an understanding, Lisa gave them both a long-suffering look. "Okay, okay." She pointed a finger at Heather. "But before I say a word, Heather-my-friend, you are going to *swear* to me that when all this is settled, you'll sit down very calmly with me and tell me the entire story! Promise?"

"Promise." Heather smiled. "Now, tell me about Adam. Is he all right? Did you make him understand that I just wanted to be alone for a while, that I'd come back?"

"At first"—Lisa sighed—"I thought it was just a lovers' quarrel, but Adam was so upset that it worried me. The first few weeks he practically haunted this place. Daddy had decided to stay here until you came back, and Adam was none too pleased about that. He asked me every morning at the office if I'd heard from you, and I kept telling him that you'd come back when you were ready. He showed up here at odd hours, demanding to know if we'd heard anything.

"He wouldn't get a replacement for you at the office, so he used girls from the typing pool, and none of them lasted for more than a few days. He started losing his temper and snapping at everyone, particularly whatever poor kid happened to be sitting behind your desk." Lisa shook her head with a grimace. "He's been impossible, Heather. The entire staff has been walking on eggshells and talking in whispers."

Heather was a little pale. "I should have called," she murmured. "I never meant to worry him."

With a sigh Lisa went on. "I have to admit that I was a bit impatient with him. Like I said, I thought it was just a quarrel. And then Daniel Blake came here this morning, and I realized why Adam was so worried. I mean, he'd already lost you once, for God's sake! Anyway, I decided that I'd better talk to him again and convince him that you hadn't run away for good.

"Well, he hasn't been at the office all this week, and no one had the nerve to find out why. He's called every night to ask if I've heard from you, but he didn't sound like himself, and that worried me. So after Mr. Blake left this morning, I went over to Adam's apartment. The houseman let me in when I told him who I was."

Lisa hesitated, and then went on quietly. "Adam looks terrible, Heather, as if he hasn't eaten or slept in days. He was just sitting in the living room, staring at that painting of you. He was drinking, from the looks of him. But he wasn't drunk. He jumped up as soon as I came in, but when he realized that I couldn't tell him anything more that I already had told him, he looked—I don't know"— Lisa made a helpless gesture—"empty, defeated."

With no awareness of doing so, Heather rose to her feet. "I have to go to him," she murmured almost inaudibly.

Leon started to get up. "I'll drive you."

"No." She shook her head with a smile. "Thank you, Leon, but I'll take a cab."

Smiling a little wryly, Leon settled back on the couch. "I had a feeling," he murmured, "that you'd say that."

CHAPTER TEN

When Douglas opened the door of Adam's apartment, his expression showed first surprise, and then heartfelt relief. "Miss Heather! I mean, Miss Richards." For once the normally impassive houseman was clearly off balance.

Heather smiled as she stepped into the apartment. "It's all right, Douglas. I've got my memory back now."

Douglas closed the door behind her, looking, if possible, even more relieved. "If I may say so, Miss Heather, I am most glad to hear that."

She glanced down the long hall to the studio door. "Is he . . . ?"

The houseman shook his head. "He won't go into the studio, Miss Heather. He's in the living room and . . . he isn't well."

Heather stared toward the closed double doors for a long moment and then turned to Douglas with a faintly teasing smile. "Douglas, do you think you could find yourself a date and disappear for a day or two?"

The middle-aged man's lips twitched faintly. "I can do better than that, Miss Heather. My sister lives in Oakland,

and she's been pestering me to come and spend a week or so with her family."

"They say Oakland's lovely this time of year." Heather smiled.

"I believe I'll find out if that's true." He bowed slightly, his eyes fairly twinkling. "If you will excuse me, Miss Heather, I'll just go call my sister and pack. I—er—I'll let myself out."

Still smiling, Heather watched as he disappeared through the kitchen, heading for his room. Then, with a deep breath, she walked down the hallway to the living room. She hesitated at the doors, uncertain for the first time. One question tormented her, just as it had tormented her all during the early months of her marriage to Adam, just as it had tormented her when she had regained her memory.

If Adam loved her, why had he never told her so?

Fiercely she pushed the question away and opened the doors, stepping inside the living room and closing them behind her. Adam was sitting a few feet away, his chair turned to face the portrait hanging in lonely splendor on one wall.

He was unshaven, his black hair rumpled, as though he had spent a great deal of time running his fingers through it. His jeans were creased, his shirt wrinkled and unbuttoned, his feet bare. The long, sensitive fingers of one hand wrapped around a brandy snifter. An empty bottle lay on the floor by his feet.

As the doors clicked shut, he muttered hoarsely, "Damn you, I told you to leave me alone!" He didn't look around.

Heather stepped down into the sunken living room, trembling slightly. "I will if you want me to, Adam," she said softly.

His head jerked around, the black eyes burning with exhaustion in a white face. In the dimness of the room, she must have looked like a ghost. His mouth twisted, a tormented expression gripped the pale face. He dropped the glass, his hands coming up to cover his face. A fierce shudder wracked his lean body. "Oh, *God,*" he muttered. "She keeps haunting me . . ."

Moved almost unbearably by the anguish in his voice, Heather ran forward to kneel at his feet. "Adam . . ." She clasped his wrists and gently pulled his hands down. "Adam, look at me."

Pain-filled black eyes stared down into hers for a long moment. Hesitantly his trembling fingers moved to touch her cheek. "Not a dream?"

"Not a dream." Heather was unaware of the tears coursing down her cheeks, horrified by the pain she had unintentionally caused him to suffer. She held his hand against her wet cheek and turned to kiss the rough palm. "I'm sorry. I'm sorry I ran away."

With a harsh groan Adam pulled her up onto his lap, his mouth searching blindly for hers. Their lips met in a kiss of explosive hunger, driving and urgent. He was too overwrought to be gentle, but Heather didn't ask for gentleness. He had lit a fire in her heart more than three years before, and she knew that it would take the balance of eternity for that flame to die. She wanted him. She wanted him with every fiber of her being.

She closed her eyes, her heart thudding as she felt his warm, shaking lips raining feverish kisses over her face, felt the rough scrape of his beard against her tender skin. Locking her fingers in the soft thickness of his hair, she pulled his mouth back to hers, needing him desperately.

Their mouths clung together hotly, greedy for the taste, the feel of the other. It was as if each feared that the world was about to end, and they had only these few precious seconds together.

At long last, Adam drew back far enough to rest his forehead against hers, his brandy-scented breath warm on her face. His hands moved over her slender body almost compulsively as he stared down into the deep purple of her eyes. "Oh, God, Heather," he muttered roughly, "I thought I'd lost you. I was going out of my mind!"

Heather caressed his lean face tenderly, her heart turning over as her fingers explored the lines of pain and despair. "What have you been doing to yourself?" she whispered huskily. "You look so tired."

A brief glimmer of amusement lit the dark eyes. "I look like hell," he said thickly. "I haven't had a bath or a shave in days. I'm not even fit to touch you, but . . ." The expression in his eyes said plainly that he was afraid to let her go. She had never seen him so vulnerable, all his proud assurance stripped away.

Aching with love for him, Heather wriggled from his lap and tugged gently at his hand. "Come with me," she invited softly.

Adam rose to his feet, swaying unsteadily, his black eyes fixed on her face. "Where?"

Heather started leading him toward the bedroom, throwing a half-teasing, half-seductive look over her shoulder at him. "I'll scrub your back if you'll scrub mine," she offered lovingly.

Never taking his eyes from her, Adam followed as she led him down the short hallway, through the bedroom, and into the master bath. He stood, trancelike, watching as she turned on the shower and then came back to him to push the shirt off his shoulders. She felt his heart beating heavily in his chest, muscles tightening as she ran her hands over them. With a sultry little smile, purple fire in her eyes, she stepped back and kicked off her sandals, beginning to unbutton her blouse.

She held his eyes with her own, completely unselfconscious as she stripped before him, her only desire to wipe the strained, careworn expression off his face. As the last dainty scrap of lace hit the floor, her expression melted into laughter, and she turned toward the shower stall, saying teasingly over her shoulder, "You've fallen behind!"

A sudden grin crossed Adam's face as he watched her disappear behind the smoked glass, and his hands shook slightly as they reached for the waistband of his jeans.

Seconds later he joined her in the stall.

Warm water cascaded over them and laughter filled the narrow stall. But every teasing kiss, every caress, only intensified the sharp, driving edge of the desire they felt for each other. It was like a fever in their blood simmering just beneath the boiling point, just under control.

They dried each other with fluffy towels, their movements becoming languid, the teasing laughter falling away from them. Heather wrapped a towel around her, conscious of his passionate eyes following her every movement, breathless beneath the intensity of his look. She pushed her wet hair over her shoulder and gave him a smile. "You got my hair all wet. Now I'll have to borrow your dryer again." There was a betraying huskiness in her voice, and she hurried on. "And you'd better shave. You look like a pirate, and I'm deathly afraid of pirates!"

He reached out and caught her hand as she started to turn away, carrying her fingers to his lips. "I don't want to let you out of my sight," he said with soft fierceness.

Shy now as she had not been before, Heather blushed slightly, her heart racing away at the possessive note in his voice. "I'll leave the door open," she promised huskily, drawing her hand from his. With an effort that was almost painful, she turned away and went into the bedroom. She dried her hair quickly, aware that he was watching her in the mirror above the vanity as he shaved.

Darkness had fallen outside, and Heather left only the bedside lamp on as she abandoned her towel and slid between cool sheets. She turned on her side to face the open bathroom door, her eyes meeting Adam's in the mirror as he somewhat recklessly finished shaving. For a moment she felt a flicker of gratitude that the days of single-edged razors were long past, otherwise, with all the attention he was devoting to his task, Adam would surely have cut his own throat.

He turned off the bathroom light and came into the bedroom just then, moving with the peculiar, catlike grace that had always possessed the power to rivet her eyes and stop her breathing. She feasted her eyes on the lean, powerfully muscled body as Adam flung his towel toward the bathroom and slid between the sheets to join her. He made a hoarse sound under his breath as he reached for her, burying his face in her silky hair and muttering disjointedly.

"Oh, God, Heather, never leave me again! I woke up, and you were gone. I could have shot myself for not having convinced you how much you meant to me . . . looked for you all night . . . and then Lisa said you'd gone away to think. I thought you were gone for good! I kept looking for your face, listening for your voice . . ."

Heather stroked his dark hair and listened, her heart lurching when his words ended with a strange broken sound. Intuitively she knew that Adam hadn't realized she had regained her memory, but she didn't want to bring that up now. Not now, when her body was clamoring for his possession. She pulled his head up and looked at the darkly flushed face, the passionate eyes. "I love you, Adam," she whispered shakily. "I love you so much!"

He closed his eyes for a brief moment, an expression of heartfelt relief and joy smoothing away the lines of remembered pain. "Oh, God, Heather, I've waited so long to hear you say that! I love you, my darling." His eyes opened, a burning tenderness in them, and then he was lowering his head until his mouth found hers. The kiss was gentle at first, but their need was too great to allow passion

176

to build slowly. Heather felt a burning fever rage to life within her, matching the flame she could feel inside Adam. It was like nothing she'd ever felt before, as though she were flying with fiery wings. Rough hands moved over her body, scorching wherever he touched, teasing and arousing until she nearly went out of her mind. She responded to his touch with wild abandon, her own hands exploring, caressing.

She arched beneath him when his mouth found the hardened tip of her breast, a moan breaking from her lips as delight pierced her body. Half-sobbing, she cried out his name, conscious only of sweet tension building within her, every sense alive to a pleasure she had never known before. His expression locked in fierce desire, Adam groaned out her name hoarsely, muttered broken endearments.

They were two lovers alone in their own world, a world of suddenly unleashed passion so violent, so powerful, that it threatened to engulf them in its fury. It was a tempest of raging winds and churning seas, carrying them higher and higher, every kiss and caress almost brutal in its shattering intensity. They loved and fought like wild things, the hunger within them driving them to the very brink of madness, until the sheer need for physical release sent them soaring over the edge in an exploding fireball of delight.

They came back to earth slowly, reluctantly, hearts gradually returning to normal, breathing becoming steady again. With limbs still entangled, they lay in the soft lamp-glow and strove—as mortals often strive—to understand an experience that had given them both a fleeting glimpse of heaven.

"You're the only woman in the world for me, Heather," Adam murmured huskily, a thread of awe in his voice. His arms tightened around her, one hand moving to stroke her tumbled hair. "I couldn't live without you. You realize that now, don't you?"

Heather rubbed her cheek against his shoulder adoringly, her violet eyes sleepy. "I know, darling," she whispered. "And it's the same for me too."

Adam reached out to turn off the lamp and then shifted slightly to draw her more firmly into his arms. Kissing her forehead tenderly, he murmured, "My beautiful Heather, beloved."

Heather drifted off to sleep, lulled by the steady beat of his heart, content at last in the certainty of his love.

She woke the next morning to the dreamy realization that she had lain securely in Adam's arms all night. His embrace was almost fierce, even in sleep, as though he feared that she would slip away from him. She lifted her head, careful not to waken him, her breath catching at the gauntness of his face. He looked so tired!

Realizing that he had probably not eaten very much in days, she moved cautiously until she had slipped from his embrace, determined to cook him a good breakfast. He shifted restlessly as the warmth of her body left him, a faint troubled frown crossing his sleeping face. Pausing only to tenderly brush back a lock of black hair that had fallen onto his forehead, Heather went to the dresser and rummaged about until she found one of Adam's pajama tops. It was ridiculously large for her, and she had to smile as she rolled back the sleeves.

With a singing heart she entered the kitchen. It took nearly an hour to prepare breakfast, and by the time she was finished, she was fighting hunger pangs of her own. She found a lap tray in the pantry and loaded it down, so much so that she nearly staggered when she lifted it. *Enough to feed an army!* she thought, and laughed at the memories that thought brought to mind.

Adam was sitting up in bed when she entered the room, a flickering wildness in his eyes. He was staring around, his features tense with anxiety, every muscle in his body rigid. As soon as he saw her he slumped, the tension draining from him. "God," he muttered hoarsely, "I thought you'd gone. Or that I had dreamed the whole thing. I don't know which I dreaded worse."

Heather hurried over to place the tray across his lap and climb into bed beside him. Leaning against him, she lifted her face for his kiss, violet eyes glowing. "I'm here, darling. And it was no dream," she murmured against his lips. She giggled suddenly as she drew away from him and picked up a slice of bacon from the tray. "And I've got the aching muscles to prove it, you brute!" Her eyes teased him as she nibbled the bacon.

Adam smiled in response as he picked up a fork, but his eyes were worried. "I didn't hurt you, did I?" he asked gruffly. "I tried to be gentle, darling, but . . ."

She reached to touch his cheek fleetingly, a tender smile curving her mouth. "You didn't hurt me, Adam. I promise you that." The expression in his eyes nearly stopped her heart, so full of love that it was almost painful. She watched as he turned his gaze to the tray and began eating, laughed and accepted when he turned to gravely offer her a bite. Laughing, teasing one another, they rapidly cleared the tray of every bite of food.

Later Adam set the tray on the floor by the bed and turned to look at her searchingly. "You're different," he murmured almost to himself. "More open. Before, you were—" His voice broke off abruptly, an expression of uncertainty crossing his face.

Quietly Heather said, "Before, I was afraid of you." When he looked startled, she went on softly, "Three years ago."

Adam closed his eyes briefly. "You've remembered," he sighed.

Gently she said, "I remembered the night I ran away from here. I went into your studio and everything came back to me. When I saw the paintings. That's why I ran."

Worry tightened his face. "Heather, I didn't have anything to do with those divorce papers, I swear! I could have killed my father when I came home and found—"

Heather placed a finger over his lips, cutting off the flow of impassioned words. "I know that, darling. But don't blame Daniel too much. I never would have run away if I hadn't been uncertain to begin with."

He stared at her, eyes intent. "But why were you uncertain? And just now, you said that you were afraid of me. How could that be, Heather? You knew I loved you."

"No."

"What do you mean, no?" He looked astonished.

She gave him a wry little smile. "Daniel was right about one thing: I was too young for you."

Adam's lips thinned. "No," he said flatly.

"Yes," Heather said quietly, insistently. "Darling, I was too young. Oh, not in years. I was too young emotionally. I knew that you wanted me, but I was always afraid that you didn't love me—because you had never said that you did."

He ran a hand through his hair almost nervously, his eyes distracted. "It never seemed adequate somehow," he muttered thickly, "just to say 'I love you.' From the first moment I set eyes on you at that gallery, I knew that I'd been waiting for you all my life. Until that day, I'd never felt real. It was as if I was half alive, and then I met you and I was whole for the first time."

Softly Heather said, "It all happened too fast. I loved you, but I was frightened by the way you made me feel." A teasing glint entered her eyes. "I was trying to test the water with one toe, and you pulled me in before I could even get my bathing suit on!"

He grinned, and then the grin faded. "I was obsessed," he said on a low, driven note. "I knew you were young, innocent. That knowledge just increased my obsession for you, deepened it. I was afraid to tell you how I felt, afraid I'd overwhelm you, frighten you. And then when you found out exactly who I was, I could see how disturbed you were. You tried to stop seeing me, and that terrified me. I told myself that I'd lose you unless I acted, so I stampeded you into marrying me."

"And frightened me even more." Her smile was a little sad. "If I had just let myself feel, everything would have been so different. But I was so afraid of getting hurt, so afraid that you'd get tired of me, that I just kept pushing the feelings away. The only time I could really let go . . ." Her eyes closed suddenly, a soft blush creeping up in her cheeks.

"The only time you really let go," Adam said deeply, "was in my arms at night. We were so busy making love, we never really talked to each other." After a moment he said quietly, "Tell me about the accident. It's been haunting me ever since I found out."

She looked down at the bracelet on her wrist. "Before I tell you about that, tell me how you found me."

He frowned slightly, then shrugged. "It isn't very complicated. I had been planning on expanding the company to the West Coast, mainly because I wanted to get away from New York. I had some people checking into firms out here when Norden passed the word that he wanted to sell. The lawyers were taking care of all the paperwork, and they sent a list of Norden employees to New York, along with some other information. Your name was on the list.

"God, I've never felt such relief! Just knowing where you were, and that you were all right. I dumped everything into David's lap and caught the first plane out here." He looked down at her with a faint grimace. "I drove by your apartment at least a dozen times, but I couldn't get up the nerve to go in. You were living under your maiden name, and I didn't know about the memory loss. I was afraid that you wouldn't see me."

He sighed. "The rest was pure luck. Andrews—remember him?—knew me from New York. He came by here and saw the painting of you, knew that I'd done it. He's one of the few people who know that I paint. Anyway, he asked to exhibit it, and since I was counting on seeing you soon, I let him take it. He called me the next day to say that a Leon Masters had been asking him questions about the painting and the artist. Masters had told him that he knew the girl in the painting, that she had lost her memory and that the portrait might help her to remember."

Heather smiled slightly. "And you were there when Leon took me to see the painting."

Adam nodded. "The memory loss threw me. I didn't know whether I should tell you about us. So I decided to take things slowly."

"Slowly?" She started laughing. "Is that how you'd describe that . . . that attack of yours? I thought you were out of your mind!"

With a faint grin Adam said, "I needed to make you aware of me. That war—it was a spur-of-the-moment idea. But it backfired on me." He looked at her wryly. "The first weapon you pulled out of your pocket was Alex Sinclair— playboy of the Western World! Scared the hell out of me when you left the office with him. I sat outside his apartment for an hour in cold sweat, terrified of what might have been happening inside."

"No wonder you were so upset," Heather murmured, "talking about your 'right' to know my every move, but it still didn't make sense to me. If I had remembered being your wife . . ."

With a sigh Adam murmured, "That was the problem —you didn't remember. I nearly told you, but I was afraid the shock would be too much for you. So I fought every instinct urging me to just grab you and carry you off somewhere."

"Why didn't you just tell me that you loved me?"

"Would you have believed me?" he replied dryly.

Heather reflected for a moment and then nodded. "You're probably right. I didn't trust you." She smiled suddenly. "Those flowers were messages, weren't they?"

He grinned. "I was dropping hints all over the place, but you never seemed to react to them. The flowers, that comment about your unearthly beauty."

"Now, that one I reacted to," Heather said immediately. "That phrase bothered me, and I couldn't understand why. You used to drive me up the wall saying that! Lisa said it once, teasing me, and a bell went off in my head." She looked at him wryly. "And how about that cute little message you asked Lisa to pass along to me?"

"I thought that would get to you!" he laughed.

"Get to me?" Heather shook her head. "Half of me was relieved that you hadn't lost interest, and the other half wanted to strangle you for pulling such a sneaky, under-handed trick!"

He looked innocent. "What do you mean, sneaky? All's fair, you know. Besides, I was just punishing myself. I had to act indifferent in the office, and all the time my blood pressure was going through the roof. That's why I finally caved in the night of the dinner party. I tried my damndest to convince you that I cared." He sighed softly. "But you didn't trust me."

She reached up fleetingly to touch his cheek. "That was the night I realized that I loved you. And that's when the real battle began. I wanted to give in to you so badly that I ached inside, but I kept asking myself how I'd feel when you grew tired of me and walked away."

He looked at her with tender eyes. "I could never walk away from you, sweet Heather. How far would I get with-out the other half of myself?"

She threw her arms around his neck, burying her face against the strong column of his throat, feeling the fine silver chain of the medallion against her chin, the medal-lion that she had given him on his birthday shortly after

183

their marriage. Her mind's eye saw the inscription: TO MY DARLING HUSBAND. LOVE, HEATHER. If she had only seen it sooner! "I love you, Adam," she whispered.

His arms tightened around her as he lowered her to the pillows, raining gentle kisses over her face. "And I love you, sweet Heather," he murmured huskily. He raised his head, looking down at her softly flushed face. "The accident," he prompted quietly.

Heather toyed with the medallion, avoiding his intent gaze. "You were so cruel to me in your car that night," she murmured, still putting off the final revelation.

He was silent for a moment, then accepted the change of subject. "I was nearly out of my mind that night," he confessed thickly. "I needed you so badly and it was so perfect. And then, all of a sudden, you weren't with me anymore, and I didn't know why. And when you said that you wouldn't let me use you, something snapped. I didn't mean all the things I said, baby. I'm sorry."

The endearment vividly brought to mind the one thing she had been unable to tell him, and Heather almost winced.

"Heather—"

"You haven't asked me about Leon," she interrupted him quickly, and he allowed the detour once again, although she could feel a growing tension in him.

"I've been afraid to. From the moment I saw him with you in the gallery, I knew that he was in love with you. I saw the way he looked at you, at the painting. He's . . . important to you, isn't he?"

She looked up at him, her violet eyes soft. "Yes. He's been very good to me, Adam. But he knows how I feel about you, and how you feel about me. He said that he'd been getting over me ever since he saw the painting, that it convinced him there was a man in my past who cared very much."

Adam smiled slightly. "I had a feeling that he'd guessed

at least part of the truth the night you ran away. Neither one of us was making much sense that night, but I gathered that he knew you had run away from me once before."

Heather's eyes flickered with amusement. "Lisa said that the two of you nearly came to blows."

He grimaced. "We probably would have if we both hadn't been so worried about you. Needless to say, we were not very polite."

Her gaze dropped to the medallion again, and she fingered it absently. "He took care of me after the accident," she told her husband quietly. "It was pure luck, his being at that Indiana hospital when they brought me in. No one knew who I was, and I couldn't tell them. I had run off without my purse. All I had was the money in my pockets, and that I spent on gas for the car. The only thing the authorities knew was my first name, because I was wearing the bracelet.

"Leon took me to his private hospital in Colorado, assumed responsibility for me. He's a plastic surgeon," she went on, and then added quickly as Adam stiffened, "I wasn't at his hospital because of that though."

Adam touched the tiny scar on her cheek with unsteady fingers. "You have to tell me, Heather," he said gently. "Whatever it is that you're hiding, you have to tell me. We can't have it between us for the rest of our lives, sweetheart."

"I know." She lifted dark purple eyes to meet his. "Will you promise me something, Adam?"

He frowned slightly. "I'd promise you the universe if I thought I could deliver. What is it, Heather?"

"Forgive Daniel."

His jaw tightened. "Three years. Three *years*, Heather!" His black eyes were intense. "How can I forget that? I lived in hell for three years because of him!"

She cradled his hand against her cheek, looking at him

pleadingly. "He's so sorry for what he did, Adam! He talked to me yesterday and—"

"Talked to you?" Adam frowned again. "He's in San Francisco? How did he find you?"

"I was staying at Norden's house. He and his wife have gone on a cruise. Daniel came by hoping that Norden might know where I was. He had seen my name on a list of Norden employees. He wanted to find me and tell me that it was he, and not you, who broke us up. But I already knew that. We talked for a long time. He's changed, Adam."

"I don't believe that," Adam said flatly. "He wouldn't change if it was his last hope into heaven."

"Darling," Heather said softly, "I'd be the last person in the world to believe it if it wasn't true, but it is. Losing your love and respect has torn him up inside!"

"I hope he's in agony," Adam responded harshly.

She touched the taut line of his jaw with tender fingers. "You don't mean that. Adam, the past is past. Let it be over. Please."

He looked down at her for a long moment and then groaned softly, his face relaxing. "I can't refuse you anything! But I won't make a promise I might not be able to keep. So I promise to try. Will that do?" When she hesitated, he said quietly, "It's the only promise I can make, Heather. I'll try."

"I just don't want you to blame Daniel for the accident or . . . or anything else. I was driving too fast and the road was slippery. If it was anyone's fault, it was my own."

His body was tense. He knew that whatever she had to tell him would not be easy to bear. "Tell me, Heather."

She gazed at him with remembered pain shimmering in her eyes. "There's no easy way to say it." Taking a deep breath, she said very quietly, "I was pregnant, Adam. I lost the baby in the accident."

His face drained of color, the black eyes going opaque.

186

"Oh, God," he muttered, burying his face in her hair. "Our child! Heather, I'm so sorry! My poor darling!" He lifted his head suddenly, the black eyes blazing. "My father has a lot to answer for," he bit out tautly.

"No." Heather framed his lean face with gentle hands. "You made me a promise, darling, and I'm going to hold you to it. You must try to forgive Daniel. We can't let the past poison the future."

Slowly the black rage drained from his eyes. He nodded his head slightly, accepting the truth of her words. "I'll keep my promise," he told her huskily. "But it won't be easy."

"Nothing worthwhile ever is," she responded softly.

"So wise," he murmured almost inaudibly. "What did I ever do to deserve you, sweet Heather?" His expression was very tender. "I must have had a very good fairy at my christening."

"Speaking of christenings," Heather said softly, her violet eyes glowing, "how do you feel about becoming a father?"

He went very still, staring down at her with a look of growing wonder in his eyes. "A baby?" He swallowed hard. "Really?"

"Really." A smile of incredible beauty spread across her face. "In about seven and a half months, you're going to become a father."

"Darling . . ." Feverish lips rained soft kisses over her smiling face, strong arms held her gently, close to his heart. "Dear God, I love you so much!"

When his lips moved gently over hers, Heather gave herself up to the wonder of his love, dimly aware that there would be time for the other explanations, time to tell him why she'd stayed away so long, and how Daniel had brought her to her senses. But right now the only thing she was conscious of was the growing need to belong to him again.

"Make love to me, darling," she whispered against his lips.

Adam answered by pulling her close. "My love," he murmured. Then his eyes became worried. "The baby? I don't want to hurt either of you, sweetheart. Are you sure it's safe?"

"It's perfectly safe." Her eyes teased him. "If you think, Adam Blake, that I'm going to stay on my own side of the bed for seven and a half months just because I'm going to have your baby, you'd better think again!"

"Wanton," he muttered hoarsely. "What am I going to do with you?"

She wound her arms around his neck, trembling at the feel of his hand sliding warmly, possessively, over her still-flat stomach.

He laughed unsteadily, his lips at her throat. "You're incredible, sweet witch," he told her gruffly, giving a stifled gasp as her teasing fingers slid down the length of his spine. "Lord, what you do to me!"

"What you do to me," she whispered just before his lips captured hers, "is drive me out of my mind!" Her breath filling his mouth, she added huskily, "But what a sweet madness it is."

Anyone would think a woman had never had a baby before! Heather thought with tender amusement as Adam placed pillows behind her back and perched on the arm of her chair with a worried frown.

"Are you sure you're all right, sweetheart?" he asked anxiously, putting a comforting arm around her shoulders. "It was a long flight. Maybe you should lie down for a while."

"I'm fine, Adam," she responded gently, looking up at him with a loving smile. "As a matter of fact, I think I'll survive this last month better than you will!" Her eyes teased him softly.

188

David Blake, from his lounging position on the couch, laughed in amusement. "Don't worry, Heather," he assured his sister-in-law blandly, "I'll hold his hand while you're in the delivery room."

"You won't have to." Her violet eyes swung to meet the bright blue eyes of Adam's brother. "He'll be with me."

David choked as his drink apparently went down the wrong way, and gazed at his brother with watering, awed eyes. "You've got more guts than I have, old man," he managed finally.

Adam smiled down at his wife with tender eyes. "I want to be with her every minute," he said softly.

Heather smiled up at him and cradled his hand against her cheek for a brief moment, then turned her gaze once again to her young brother-in-law. She had met him only two months before, when he had flown out to California to take a look at the West Coast branch of the family business, and an immediate rapport had sprung up between them.

He had the family good looks, inheriting blue eyes from his mother and dark coloring from Daniel, and a sinful amount of charm. At twenty-two he had already decided that the advertising business would be his life, claiming that the only artistic talent he possessed was the ability to pick the right wine for dinner. Having seen some of his sketches, Heather knew that to be untrue, but she also knew that David lacked the artistic genius that drove his older brother.

"How do you think you'll like living in California, David?" she asked, since it had already been decided that David would take over the company Adam had bought.

With a soulful sigh David replied, "Well, I'll sure as hell like the women! Maybe I'll get lucky like Adam and find myself a sweet California girl who'll help me mend my ways."

Adam laughed. "You'll be very, very lucky if you find

189

one like Heather. When they made her, they broke the mold!"

"Just my luck," David said morosely, and then brightened abruptly. "Hey, by the way, what's my little niece or nephew going to be called?"

Heather's eyes turned suddenly to Daniel, standing silently by the fireplace. The atmosphere between Adam and his father had been strained since they had arrived, moments ago, here in the house where Adam had grown up. Aside from polite hellos, they had exchanged not one word, and she wondered worriedly if she had been wrong in urging Adam to see his father for the first time in three years.

But she couldn't bear to allow the rift between them to continue. She had talked to Daniel often during the past months, calling him to tell him about the baby at first, and then calling simply because she felt a growing fondness for her father-in-law.

He was, like his son, a complicated man, but she felt that she understood him, and the only thing needed to make her happiness complete was to see him and Adam on good terms again. Adam, however, had proven difficult, finding it almost impossible to forgive his father. She had done her best to make him believe that Daniel was truly sorry, urging him to forget the bitterness of the past.

Heather was painfully aware that this could possibly be the only chance for Adam to openly forgive his father. They were stopping here in New York only for the night, and going on to Vermont and the farm that had been left to Adam by his grandmother. It had taken all of her persuasion to get Adam to cross his father's threshold once. She was unsure of her ability to perform the same feat twice.

And how would Adam answer his brother's question?

She looked up at him to find his black eyes brooding down on her, the expression in them unfathomable. She

190

met his look with soft pleading and hope in her own eyes. The look held for a long time, and then Adam glanced at his brother.

"If the baby's a girl, we're going to call her Kathleen, after Heather's mother."

David's blue eyes flicked to Heather's strained face, her eyes fixed imploringly on the unyielding profile of her husband. "And if it's a boy?" he asked quietly.

Adam's eyes returned to his wife's face. The hand resting on her shoulder lifted to touch her cheek gently, and then a faint, rueful smile twisted his lips. "If it's a boy . . ." He looked across at his father's quiet figure, met the baffled black eyes with a new expression of understanding. "If it's a boy," he said quietly, directly to his father, "our son will be named Daniel."

Daniel's eyes seemed to cloud over as he read and understood the expression of forgiveness in the matching eyes of his son. His throat moved on a painful swallow, and he lifted his glass in a toast, his gaze dropping to the glowing face of his daughter-in-law.

"To Heather," he said huskily, "and the next generation of Blakes."

Adam looked down at the turned up face of his wife, toasting her with his eyes. "To my love," he added softly.

With a cockeyed grin tugging at the corners of his mouth, David lifted his own glass in a salute. "To those incredible California girls," he said with irrepressible humor. "Long may they reign!"

LOOK FOR NEXT MONTH'S
CANDLELIGHT ECSTASY ROMANCES™